THE STORM

JACQUELYN AEBY

THORNDIKE
CHIVERS

This Large Print edition is published by Thorndike Press, Waterville, Maine USA and by BBC Audiobooks Ltd, Bath, England.

Thorndike Press is an imprint of Thomson Gale, a part of The Thomson Corporation.

Thorndike is a trademark and used herein under license.

The text of this Large Print edition is unabridged.

Other aspects of the book may vary from the original edition.

Set in 16 pt. Plantin.

LIBRARY OF CONGRESS CATALOGING-IN-PUBLICATION DATA

Aeby, Jacquelyn.
    The storm / by Jacquelyn Aeby.
        p. cm. — (Thorndike Press large print candlelight)
    ISBN 0-7862-9178-8 (alk. paper)
        1. Women editors — Fiction. 2. Authors and publishers — Fiction. 3.
    Winter storms — Fiction. 4. Large type books. I. Title.
    PS3557.R3338S76 2006
    813'.54—dc22   2006028607

BRITISH LIBRARY CATALOGUING-IN-PUBLICATION DATA AVAILABLE

U.S. Hardcover: ISBN 13: 978-0-7862-9178-6; ISBN 10: 0-7862-9178-8
U.K. Hardcover: 978 1 405 63984 2 (Chivers Large Print)
U.K. Softcover: 978 1 405 63985 9 (Camden Large Print)

Published in 2006 in the U.S. by arrangement with
Maureen Moran Agency.
Published in 2007 in the U.K. by arrangement with the author.

Printed in the United States of America on permanent paper
10 9 8 7 6 5 4 3 2 1

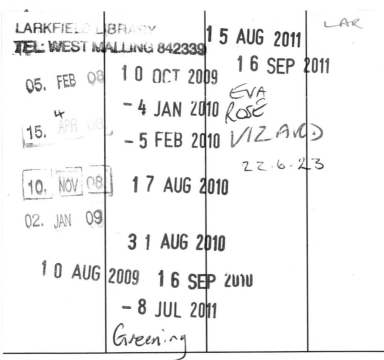
Please return on or before the latest date above.
You can renew online at *www.kent.gov.uk/libs*
or by telephone 08458 247 200

LP
01/08.

AEBY, J
THE STORM
C153181652

CUSTOMER SERVICE EXCELLENCE

Libraries & Archives

Kent
County
Council

00884\DTP\RN\07.07   LIB 7

THE STORM

CHAPTER ONE

Alison Monroe drew the powerful car onto the shoulder of the highway to check her map. She had plenty of time, and in fact she would probably arrive early for her appointment, but she could not afford to take a chance on making a wrong turn. She suspected that Jonathan Warwick would not listen to excuses.

Ah, here she was, halfway between Sitwell and Athens. She followed the blue line with her finger until she found the right turnoff for Crockett. Repeating the directions under her breath until she had them firmly established in her mind, she tossed the map onto the seat beside her and pulled out onto the road again.

The car handled superbly, and she was grateful to Paul for lending it to her for the trip. But, she smiled to herself, why not? If she managed to get Jonathan Warwick's signature on the contract she had in her attaché case, it would be a lifesaver for Danvers Publishing, of which her employer, Paul Danvers, was president.

She drove swiftly and tried not to think about the manuscript whose first five chapters also rested in her case, tucked behind the front seat. The memoirs bore an uneasy resemblance to a ticking bomb, and she hoped she wouldn't be too close when it went off. But it was her own discovery, and if Jonathan Warwick chose to reveal, spitefully and at length, all the foibles, or worse, of the colleagues he had met during a long and often misspent life in the upper echelons of society, it was his fault, not hers.

All she'd had to do was read that manuscript when he had first sent it to Danvers to recognize, in her capacity as junior editor, that here was something!

Well, all that lay in the past, or, in the case of the rest of the manuscript, in the future. Right now she gave herself up to the pleasure of driving Paul's big car, and of looking from time to time at the unfamiliar scenery that she was passing.

Hills, rounded and gentle, many crowned with groves of trees, were bare now against the gray sky of late December. The intimate landscape closed in protectively around her. The road, now that she had left the state highway — from blue line to black-and-white checked on the map — was narrow and rounded in the middle. She cast an anxious glance at the heavy sky. She would not wish to drive these uneven roads in a snowstorm, and she had promised Paul that she would be back in time for Christmas.

And perhaps Christmas would mean something more this year. Just this morning when Paul had turned his car keys over to her, he kissed her for the first time. "You're lovelier every day," he had said softly. "Hurry back."

Perhaps —

Abruptly, she came upon the large concrete gatepost with the round cement ball on top, the one Jonathan Warwick had described in his letter inviting her up to bring him the contract for his memoirs. She must keep her wits about her now, and stop dreaming about Paul.

She slowed, expecting the gates to appear on her right, but a simple wire farm fence paralleled the road for what seemed to be an unreasonably long distance. Could she have missed anything as large as a gate? True, the afternoon was nearly gone and twilight blurred objects before her, but gates — ?

At last she saw them and slowed to a

crawl. She had an urban dislike for ditches that were merely dark shadows, too close to the road for comfort.

She turned carefully between the gate-posts, and for the first time felt misgivings diminishing her confidence. Ordinarily she could cope with anything — for example, fighting for the Warwick manuscript all the way up to a full board meeting yesterday. But this!

This was a winding road through dark shrubbery and trees that vaulted up to the skies like the supporting pylons of a cathedral. She felt dwarfed by the rampant growth, which seemed actively antagonistic, even though most of the leaves had fallen before the onslaught of winter.

She cautiously urged the car forward, following the gray driveway which glistened with frost under the headlights.

It was hard to judge how far she had traveled from the public road. She glanced fearfully to her left into the obscurity at the side of the driveway and could not repress a slight shudder. Give her the pavements and the streetlights, every time.

When she looked ahead of her again, she caught sight of movement on the opposite side of the driveway. She could not believe her eyes. She could *not* have seen something purple, shiny, and running.

Without thinking, she touched the brakes sharply. She knew instantly that she had made a mistake.

The blacktop of the driveway was slick with frost, and the car reacted violently. She fought the wheel, envisioning Paul's elegant car wrapped around the trunk of the tree looming ahead of her. The rough ground at the side of the drive eventually slowed her, and the car stopped short of disaster. The headlights picked out the seamed bark of the giant tree in greater detail than she liked. So close!

Her reaction to fright was a flood of anger. Whatever the purple thing was, what a stupid thing to do — to loom into her headlights and disappear!

She gritted her teeth and prepared to teach — whatever it was — a lesson.

She switched off the headlights, and the sudden darkness stifled her temper a bit. But she had always been impulsive, and she merely leaned against the car until her eyes grew accustomed to the darkness.

As soon as she could distinguish one object from another, she left the car and made her way into the undergrowth. Searching for something purple and shiny, she was propelled for a few yards by indignation.

Then anger treacherously disappeared and left her with only cold uneasiness.

Her steps faltered to a halt. How could she see anything in this darkness? She turned to make her way back to the car. She found an unaccountable lump, possibly of fear, in her throat. Always a realist, she told herself she was a reckless idiot. And she hoped that was the extent of it.

Her hopes were shattered when she turned and found that she did not know where she was. In vain she looked for the car. There was nothing to see but bare bushes and tree trunks, pressing as closely as the walls of a telephone booth.

Panic fluttered inside her and she suppressed a scream, stifling it to a sound that was unpleasantly like a whimper. She pushed blindly through waist-high branches, stiff and brittle.

And then, only a few feet from her where the brush gave way to a clearing, she saw a tall shape in the obscurity.

"What are you doing here?" His deep voice grated her exposed nerves.

In two steps he had crossed the distance between them and took her by the arm. "Are you all right?" he asked in a tone of voice totally different from his challenge. "Here, come out where I can see you."

In a moment, his fingers still hard on her arm, she had recovered enough to take a deep breath and prepare to do battle.

"I'm not going to hurt you," the man said, reading her thoughts. "But what are you doing here?"

She was too shaken to tell the truth. "I'm looking for something purple that ran."

Her captor seemed to undergo a sort of convulsion, and she peered suspiciously at him until she realized that he was shaken by nothing more serious than silent laughter. Unwillingly, she joined him. "I suppose it sounds silly," she said at last.

"That, at least, is the truth," he told her.

"But I did see something purple," she protested angrily. "I'm not making it up."

"Of course you're not," he said in a maddeningly soothing tone. "Something purple," he added thoughtfully, "and it ran. Six feet tall and scaly, I suppose, with a shaggy tail?"

"You don't believe me!"

"Now did I say that?"

"Oh!" she gasped in righteous indignation, and whirled to return to her car.

He released her arm and stood back. "How did you get here?"

"In a car," she said frostily, "which I nearly

13

wrecked when the — thing — frightened me."

"Really?" He took a step closer and she looked up at him. He was very tall. His eyebrows were straight black bars across his face. He was younger than she had supposed, but she wasn't sure how she knew that — perhaps from the great strength in his fingers, she decided, rubbing her arm.

"Here," he said swiftly, "I'll take you back to your car. Where are you bound for? Perhaps I can put you on the right road."

As he spoke, he took her arm again, this time more gently, and guided her through paths he seemed to know well. She could see no path, but the way was easy underfoot, and in a short time — far shorter than the time it had taken her to fight her lone way through the underbrush — they stood on the verge of the driveway.

"My car's down —" She looked about her in dismay. "I don't know which way to go. I'm turned around."

"There it is," he said at last. "Look, you can see the faint reflection on the metal."

"I can't see it."

"You're not used to the country, are you?" he said in a conversational tone. "It takes experience, I suppose, to see in the dark."

He led her to the car and helped her into

it, letting out a low whistle when he saw the rakish and expensive lines of the vehicle.

"I thought perhaps I should offer to replace your stockings," he said cheerfully, "but I see that you can afford another pair."

She could think of nothing to say to that, so she switched on the engine and the headlights. In the reflected glow she looked at him. "Thank you for getting me out of there," she said.

In the improved light she saw that his hair grew down in a perfect widow's peak over the straight eyebrows. His chin was strong — perhaps even stubborn — and for some reason she was glad to see the last of him.

"The road's too narrow to turn here," he told her. "Go up to the house and you'll find a turn-around, to help you head straight out again."

She nodded her thanks. She saw no reason to tell him that the house was her destination. It was none of his business. Her normal confidence had returned now that she was safe inside the car again.

He was laughing in that silent way that she found intensely annoying. "Be careful," he advised, his voice muffled in mirth, "and watch out for purple things."

From a corner of her memory she pulled a swift impression of the running object and remembered something she hadn't mentioned before. "It wore a green turban," she said coolly, and drove off with satisfaction, increased by the glance in her side mirror that showed him staring after her in what she hoped was astonishment.

The house, when she reached it, was aglow with lights. Its two stories generously covered a rise in ground, but it was impossible to discern its size within the dimness of the lawn.

So Jonathan wouldn't be desperate for the money they would offer for his book, she mused, and then decided that the running of such an establishment might necessitate another source of income.

She turned the car around to head it out again. She picked up her attaché case and her purse — in that order of value, she thought — and went up the broad steps to a white door with a classical fanlight above it. She lifted the knocker and let it fall back into the teeth of the bronze lion that held it.

As she waited on the porch, looking back down the driveway, she suddenly had a strange feeling that she could not identify. It seemed to be made up of several feelings: the sense of being in another land, with rolling hills confining her and shutting out the familiar world beyond; a feeling of enchantment in the tangled dimness of the grounds — where it was not unusual to see purple creatures with green turbans running riot, and strange princes springing up from the ground.

Princes! she told herself. How ridiculous! She wrenched her mind back to the world of Danvers Publishing, Paul Danvers, and the tremendously interesting and very malicious memoirs of Jonathan Warwick.

The door opened and warm air wafted out reminding her how very cold it was growing. She was grateful to step inside and feel the dark night shut out behind her. She was becoming entirely too fanciful, she told herself.

"Miss Monroe?" said the comfortable, bustling woman who had opened the door. "Mr. Warwick is resting before dinner, and asked me to take you upstairs to your room. Perhaps you would like to freshen up before dinner yourself. I'll just send Sandford to get your bag from the car. And he'll put the car away for you, if you'll just let me have your keys."

In the midst of her flow of conversation, she revealed to Alison that her name was Mrs. Gibson, that she was the cook, that Mr. Warwick always liked to meet his guests in the library before dinner, and that Alison had no more than forty-five minutes before she was due back in the library. And — Mr. Warwick liked promptness.

Insisted upon it, in fact. Mrs. Gibson made that quite clear.

Remembering the merciless way Jonathan had dissected his friends in the first hundred pages of his life story, Alison did not wish to be placed on his list of enemies. She darkly suspected that such a list would be long and comprehensive.

Forty minutes later, feeling reassured by the deep comfort of her room and the relaxing warmth of a bath, she descended the stairs. She knew that her new rose wool crepe dress made the most of her blond hair.

She hesitated in the hall, trying to decide which way to look for the library in this large and gracious house. For a moment she pictured herself and Paul together in one like it, right down to the oriental rugs on the parquet floor at her feet.

The agreeable vision faded when she heard an outburst of raised voices from her left. She moved in that direction.

There evidently were two men in the library. The one with a deep, young voice was passionately trying to convince his hearer of something.

"You'll be sorry the rest of your life," he

finished. "And I'm not sure that will be long. By the way, what was that letter you received this morning?"

The other voice was older. She guessed its owner was impervious to persuasion, or even to implied threats.

"None of your business."

"I'm not so sure. Don't tell me —" The younger man's voice sounded familiar to her all at once, perhaps because of the sudden suspicion in it. "Don't tell me you've already told people about that book! Was that your first fan letter?"

"Since you don't wish me to tell you, I won't." The older man seemed to relish the sharp exchange. With a start she realized that she was actually eavesdropping, and on a spirited family quarrel.

She moved to the open doorway of the library and cleared her throat. At the slight sound, both men wheeled to stare at her. Jonathan Warwick recovered first and advanced toward her, his hand outstretched in welcome, and introduced himself.

"Miss Monroe, how nice to meet you. I must apologize for not being on hand when you arrived, but I must have my little rest, you know." His smooth voice continued in apologies she did not hear. He led her to the deep chair nearest the fireplace, and, still talking, handed her a glass of wine.

"My nephew, Dan Warwick," Jonathan introduced his companion.

She stared at the second man, dressed, as was Jonathan, in dinner clothes. Dan returned her stare with astonished recognition. No wonder his voice had struck a familiar note. She had heard it only an hour before, in the woods.

Dan lifted his glass. "May I propose a toast, Uncle Jonathan? To you, Miss Monroe," he said, with a sketchy salute. "And to your immediate departure."

He set his glass down with slow deliberation, and left the library.

CHAPTER TWO

It was not until the next morning that Alison's indignation came off the boil. She could not remember when she had spent a worse night. Sleep had come only in the early hours of the morning, and then it was fitful and full of fleeting terrors.

There was no doubt, she realized in the hard light of a gray December morning, that Dan did not approve of his uncle's venture into autobiography. Searching her memory, his glance of dislike, verging on contempt, had come her way only when he realized that she represented Danvers Publishing. Not before.

She felt jolted, as if she had stepped into waters that were deeper than they appeared. Could Dan be right? The night had stolen her confidence in her own judgment.

She looked at her watch. Too soon to call Paul, especially if he had spent the evening with Lewis Hyde. Unwillingly, she decided that Lewis's daughter Sandra had probably been there too. And Sandra was — she could not immediately think of a word bad enough to describe Sandra. Gorgeous, with a sort of feline grace in her walk and in the way she tossed her red hair — drat Sandra!

Over breakfast coffee in the walnut-paneled dining room, she forced herself to examine her impressions of Jonathan Warwick in full daylight. Last night he had refused even to discuss the book, saying he was too fatigued. He seemed courtly, but vastly shrewd — and this was not to be wondered at.

He had been, at various times in his long life, a roving journalist, an investor in Middle East oil, and a special government emissary. Darker activities had been rumored, but never proved. He knew many of the great and the near-great of the world, all of whom he was prepared to impale on the spike of his malice. If the rest of the book bore any relation to the first five chapters —

Sandford appeared in the doorway. "Mr. Warwick would like to see you, as soon as you have finished your breakfast."

Sandford seemed to be a general handyman, valet, and whatever else anyone needed, Alison decided. She meekly fol-

22

lowed him to a room at the back of the house that she had not seen before.

If the library had been scholarly, and the dining room baronial, Mr. Warwick's study was intimate: a small room with burgundy-red carpeting and a minimum of interruption on the walls, only a single landscape, in fact. The desk was, surprisingly, an ancient rolltop painted white.

So much she noticed before she turned to Jonathan Warwick.

"Now then, Miss Monroe," he said, after a polite inquiry as to how she had slept. He rubbed his hands together. "To business. Danvers is ready to buy my little reminiscences? My bits of memory put down on paper?"

He spoke with playful modesty, but Alison had read the "bits of memory," and there was nothing humble about Jonathan.

She smiled. "The board of directors is willing to offer you a contract."

She launched into technicalities, and soon the satisfaction of knowing her way through the various terms of the document, of understanding her craft, took hold of her, and she forgot her surroundings. When at last she had finished talking about deadlines and publication schedules, she looked up to see Jonathan's reaction.

He was gazing out the window. "Has your lawyer agreed to all this?"

"Why, yes. That is, I suppose by now he will have," she faltered.

Jonathan pounced. "Lewis Hyde hasn't seen this yet?"

"No, he was out of town. Paul — Mr. Danvers, that is — was to see him last night."

She watched Jonathan carefully and detected a slight curving of the thin lips. She couldn't understand him. The terms were generous even if he didn't need the money. Looking around her, she thought wryly, I could learn to like this kind of poverty.

The question that had been on her mind for some days, in fact ever since the scandalous manuscript had crossed her desk and compelled her attention, rose insistently to her lips.

"Why did you write this book, Mr. Warwick?"

He swiveled to fix his pale blue eyes on her. "Why do you want to publish it?" he demanded in turn.

Honest with herself, at least most of the time, she knew there was only one reason: Paul Danvers. He needed a success, and she had found it for him. But she would not tell this man that. She could guess his opinion of love, and she did not wish to hear it.

"We think it would sell," she said steadily.

"And so it will." He turned to look out the window again. "Have you ever thought, Miss Monroe, about the depths of human malice?"

The question struck her unpleasantly, as though he had just read her thoughts. He didn't wait for an answer.

"The ordinary person wishes to read about the sins of his heroes. I can supply that yearning. That is all there is to it, no matter what Dan may tell you."

"Your nephew obviously disapproves."

"That need not concern us. He has no legal right to stop this book. He is really, after all, a simple soul. He doesn't appreciate the search for truth that lies in my manuscript."

Alison reflected that she didn't know any more about his reasons than she had before. She decided she didn't really like Jonathan Warwick. But then, she wasn't required to like him.

"What do you think about the contract?" she asked, breaking into his mood.

"What? Oh, the contract. I think that Lewis Hyde should see it before I say anything. You said it would be in his hands last night?"

"I believe the copy was."

"Then, Miss Monroe, I think we'll wait."

She was mystified. He didn't seem to want his own attorneys to read the contract. And it was a little surprising to her that he knew the Danvers' counsel by name. But her job was simply to get his signature on the contract. And that wasn't going to happen this morning, at any rate.

Jonathan was on his feet, concluding their discussion of the book. He favored her with the smile that must have charmed ladies in numerous world capitals. "I think that we have buried ourselves in business long enough. Now let me show you my farm."

"Farm?" It was a wrench to leave the contract unsigned and to focus her mind on real estate.

"It's not much, I admit. Just a few hundred acres, but it gives me an interest."

Sandford was passing through the hall as they emerged from the study. Jonathan asked, with a touch of irritation, "Hasn't the mail come yet?"

"No, sir," answered Sandford, with a show of consulting the hall clock. "It lacks half an hour till the usual time."

"All right, all right. When the mailman does decide to appear, come and get me, no matter where I am."

Jonathan didn't lose his edginess until they were on their way out of the house. He apologized briefly to Alison, but his mind was obviously elsewhere.

Fortunately she had brought warm clothing, she thought as they crossed the expanse of frosted lawn at the back of the house. Jonathan Warwick's hand was at her elbow, guiding her toward a complex of traditionally red buildings at the base of the slope on which the house stood.

From the grounds surrounding the large house, she realized, all these buildings and barnyards were out of sight. From Jonathan's study window, for instance, all that met the eye were a well-kept lawn, a white pergola that no doubt wore roses in the summer, and a bare-branched assortment of shrubs.

Eventually they entered a long, low building from which issued metallic clanking sounds. Inside the building there was a minimum of heat, and the pervasive, acrid smell of motor oil.

The clanking sounds came from beneath a behemoth of a vehicle that she recognized as a largescale tractor. Some convulsion seemed to be taking place in its interior, and a grimy, oil-covered man glared at their interruption.

"You remember my nephew, Dan," Jonathan said, unruffled by the unfriendly stare of the mechanic, "the one who rudely did not appear at dinner last night."

"I wouldn't have believed it," she said honestly.

"His rudeness? You would if you knew him better," Jonathan said, and she could feel the same spirit in his speech that had created the spicy tone of the manuscript back in his study.

Dan was lost to view again in the interior of the vast engine. She wanted to explain to him that she had not meant his rudeness, but only his unfamiliar appearance in coveralls and oily face, but the noise of his wrench — if that was what he was tapping with — plainly told her that he had no interest in her. Even more — that at the moment he had forgotten her existence.

She was ready to leave. She was accustomed to approval from people, and she didn't like the lonely feeling that Dan's remoteness gave her. That was all it was, she told herself — she was just spoiled. But her business was with Jonathan, not with his nephew. She turned abruptly to suggest to her host that she was ready for the next exhibit.

To her surprise, Sandford had silently appeared. When Jonathan turned to him, he said, "The mail, sir. I placed it in the study."

Jonathan lowered his voice until she could barely hear the words. "Was there anything?"

Sandford nodded slightly. With a word of apology to Alison, Jonathan followed the servant to the house — so eager to get to his study, she noted, that he passed Sandford at a near gallop. And she had thought him frail!

Suddenly she made a decision.

She walked briskly back to the tractor. By this time Dan was totally out of sight, but muffled hammering continued from the lower regions. She dropped to her hands and knees and peered at him underneath the machine. She found Dan's startling blue eyes staring back at her.

"Haven't you gone yet?" he demanded.

"Whatever happened to the jolly giant I met in the woods last night?"

"When you were chasing your purple ghost?"

"I saw something real," she protested, then, recognizing his question as a diversionary tactic, she returned to the subject at hand. "What is it you have against me?" she asked, genuine curiosity in her voice. "I haven't done a thing to you. Except," she clarified scrupulously, "to give you a certain amount of superior amusement."

He wriggled out from under the tractor and glared at her. She leaned back on her heels, her gloved hands on her knees. "My, you do look different."

"You wouldn't believe it?" he repeated her words with a sidelong, questioning glance. "But it really doesn't concern you, does it, whether I am covered with grease or wearing a dinner jacket?"

"Not in the least," she assured him. "But if I'm going to enter into a lengthy business arrangement with your uncle, I may have to come to visit, and I would merely like to know whether I will be allowed in your uncle's house, or whether you have some nasty surprise in store for me."

"Well, you do have a cool head on your shoulders. Pretty, of course. I could see that even in the darkness last night. But there's a distressing clink of metal about you — somehow makes me think of a cash register."

Recognizing an insult, she started to turn sharply on her heel and leave him alone with his bad temper. The quick gleam of triumph in his eyes stopped her. He so obviously expected her to react in just that way that she would not give him that satisfaction.

"It's easy to see you have no sense of getting ahead in the world," she taunted. "Just satisfied to work as a hired hand for your uncle? Somehow," she tilted her head to one side, "you look a little grasping yourself. Working like this to earn a place in your uncle's will?"

With that retort neatly delivered, she rose gracefully to her feet. "I must leave now," she told him with exaggerated courtesy. "I would not wish to stand between you and —" she let the implication lie in the air for a moment before she finished, "the tractor."

She had reached the sliding door of the garage before he caught up with her.

"Now that we have that out of the way," he said coldly, "I want to ask you one thing. Are you really going out on a limb with Uncle Jonathan's poisonous book?"

His eyes were extraordinarily blue, she thought randomly before she answered him. "Yes, if he'll sign the contract. And if the firm's attorney clears it."

"The firm's attorney?"

"Lewis Hyde. Paul Danvers was to see him last night. The book is borderline, I'll admit. But I think —"

What she thought was never committed to speech, for Dan was no longer listening. "What is it?"

"I think I see." He looked down at her. "You've got to leave."

"All right," she said after a moment. "I'm freezing, anyway."

"No, no. I mean leave here. Forget the book. Go away."

"That's plain enough." She felt irritation rising in her. Rude wasn't the word for him, but she couldn't think of one that would fit.

"I mean it."

"You forget I have business here. You also forget that I am your uncle's guest. Not yours."

She turned abruptly and marched out into the frosty gray morning. The chill made her gasp.

Still beside her, Dan waved toward the western horizon. "See that? There's a storm coming," he said, with a momentary change to his lazily amused manner. "You might get snowed in — with me. How would you like that?"

She glared at him and tightened her lips.

But very softly he called after her, and his tone was no longer amused. It chilled her. What he said was simple enough, and nothing she couldn't have predicted that he would say. But his words were heavy with cold determination, and something else.

She never faltered on her way back to the

house and its civilized warmth. She had no use for farm buildings, or tractors, or — she added with force — for farmers.

But she couldn't shake off the menace that Dan had sent with her.

"That book must never see the light of publication," he had said softly, but with conviction. "I will never allow it, no matter what it takes."

CHAPTER THREE

No matter what it takes!

The words developed a rhythm of their own, keeping time with her crisp footsteps on the frozen ground, hurrying when she did, slowing when she loitered. Halfway to the house she stopped. She needed time to pull herself together. Taking a deep breath that frosted her lungs, she summoned her riotous thoughts to order, before slowly continuing toward the great house looming above her.

Jonathan had certainly done well for himself. The massive house had apparently been built when solidity was more valued than style. Built of white-painted brick, it had no trim except for winter-bare ivy that struggled up the face of the building, looking like wanderings of a child's crayon.

No wonder Dan didn't want to leave a house like this for a precarious living somewhere else. With this thought, unwelcome as it was, came back the spreading chill of that unmistakable threat.

No matter what it takes!

She must telephone Paul, she decided, and buoyed up by the prospect of action, she hurried toward the house. Paul would know what to do. Besides that, she longed to hear his voice, intimate and reassuring in her ear.

She turned at the corner of the house and looked back down the hill. The garage door was closed again, and there was no sign of Dan. What did you expect? she demanded. Did you think he would follow you to the house with a pipe wrench?

The absurdity of the thought restored her to her usual good nature, and she went in by a door that seemed to be part of the kitchen. At any rate, the fragrances drifting out boded well for lunch. The door was open, and, curious as always, she stepped into the room.

Mrs. Gibson was at the far end, stirring a vast pot. Alison's greeting produced a violent reaction. Mrs. Gibson jumped, and the spoon fell from her hand and onto the spotless tile floor.

"Oh, I'm sorry!" Alison cried, as Mrs. Gibson stifled a faint scream.

"That boy!" Mrs. Gibson said obscurely

as she lowered the flame under the pot and advanced toward Alison. "Never shuts a door," she added in incomplete explanation. "The door's usually closed, miss, and you startled me."

More than that, Alison thought darkly, but she said only, "Whatever that is on the stove smells delicious. I just followed my nose."

"You're hungry," Mrs. Gibson stated. "No wonder, eating what you did for breakfast. A half a crust, that's all. Sit down."

"No, no," Alison protested reluctantly. "I must make a phone call. Collect, you know, so it won't be on your bill. May I?"

Mrs. Gibson watched her for a moment. "You're here about that man's book, aren't you." It was not a question, but Alison nodded her answer.

"What you need is a good husband to take your mind off that nasty thing."

Alison gasped in surprise.

"There, I've gone too far," Mrs. Gibson said without a hint of apology. "But I am surprised at you — such a nice girl. You can tell the old man I'm sassy, if you want to."

"I wouldn't dream of it," Alison said icily, turning on her heel. "Never mind showing me the telephone. I'll find it."

She stepped back into the entry. Straw lifted from the floor with her footsteps. Had she brought it in on her boots?

She glanced coldly at Mrs. Gibson and stepped over the straw. The housekeeper's expression was puzzling. What could she see in a few wisps of straw?

She went into the front hall, where she found Sandford standing with no apparent purpose. This was a queer household, she thought with a grimace.

In answer to her query, he suggested the library. "No one will disturb you there, Miss Monroe," he assured her.

When she paused at the open door of the empty library, she looked back to see Sandford on his hands and knees.

Jonathan was not in the library. She wondered where he had disappeared to when he had returned to the house. Remembering the study at the back of the house, she solved the question to her own satisfaction.

She closed the library door for privacy, and sat down at the enormous desk to place her call. While she idly listened to the clicks and odd, near-musical sounds that indicated the call was going through, she straightened the paper clip box on the desk, and evened it up with the leather blotter holder. By the time she had lined up the paper cutter and scissors in their tooled leather sheaths, she heard Paul's voice in her ear.

"Alison? What's the trouble? Have you got the contract signed?"

"Not yet. Paul —"

With belated caution he lowered his voice and said, "Where are you? Can you talk?"

"Yes, I can talk. Paul, there's something funny going on here."

"Funny? What do you mean?" Paul — she could see him in her mind's eye — was probably frowning at the receiver as he always did when it gave him bad news, as if the instrument itself was at fault.

Vividly she could picture him — his blond hair springing endearingly from a high forehead, his light blue eyes cold and impersonal in concentration. But they could be warm — how well she knew that!

"I mean peculiar-funny." She told him everything, except, of course, the purple thing that ran, and the meeting with Dan in the woods. She finished by saying. "This nephew — well, Paul, I wouldn't want to tangle with him."

"Tough, is he?" A note of satisfaction crept into his voice, as though at last he had something tangible to work on. "Don't you worry about him. He can't spoil it for us."

"I don't know, Paul." In spite of her efforts, her voice reflected her troubled thoughts. She would not admit to being afraid of Dan, not yet. "What shall I do?"

There was only a brief pause, the space of a breath, before he answered brusquely, "Get the contract signed. Then come back."

With that, the conversation was finished. Over. And there were no reassuringly sweet words in her ear. He is busy, busy and worried, she told herself, sitting at Jonathan's desk, still idly pushing the blotter back and forth with one finger. It was Paul's fault, she thought later, that she moved the blotter, and therefore his fault that the tiny white triangle of paper caught her eye. There was something under the blotter.

She did not intend to pry, but it was an automatic reaction. Examine the white paper. Pull it out into the open.

And then her heart stopped beating for a moment.

She held an envelope, addressed to Jonathan Warwick in large block letters. The printing was childish, and therefore somehow ominous. She shook herself mentally. She was being ridiculously fanciful.

There was no return address, but there was a postmark, smudged, illegible except for the date. December 18. Less than a week ago.

She hurriedly thrust the envelope back

under the blotter. What business was this of hers? She could not help it if her nerves were stretched taut by Dan's threat. And Paul had been no help. But he would have been, she consoled herself, if she had asked him for comfort, told him how uneasy she was.

She straightened the desk blotter again, looking to see that no telltale triangle of the envelope was visible. She could not say exactly why she dreaded the thought that someone might have seen her.

She heard a click, loud in the quiet room. Her head jerked up, but the door was closed. And then while she watched, she felt the hair rise on the back of her neck. The knob was moving!

Someone had opened the door, and someone — Sandford? Jonathan? — had watched her find the hidden envelope. And he was just now closing the door.

She flew across the room to open the door and peer into the hall. But there was no one in sight.

Suddenly she felt eyes everywhere, watching her. She wished with all her heart that she had never so much as touched the blotter. What difference did it make, anyway? An envelope, addressed in awkward printed letters. That was all.

But someone had opened the door to watch her. And closed it again without a word.

She remembered Dan's words to his uncle about a letter he had received. She remembered, too, that Jonathan wanted to be informed the moment the mail arrived. To hide away any envelopes before Dan saw them?

I have no proof that all this is tied together — the manuscript, the odd letters — she told herself. But Dan had threatened trouble, and Dan knew about at least one letter.

She looked down the hall and noticed a stray wisp of straw. She must, after all, have tracked it in on her own boots. Well, she could pick up after herself.

Even as she stopped, she knew she was simply avoiding a meeting with Jonathan. She would have to talk to him again this morning about signing the contract.

But she did not want to.

Holding the straw in her hand, she passed through the door at the back of the hall toward the kitchen. The kitchen was empty, but she could hear a voice from a room beyond it — sounding oddly familiar. She listened for a moment before she dropped the straw into a wastebasket, but she couldn't make out any words, or the identity of the speaker.

Not until she was in the hall again did she put a word to the familiar rise and fall of speech: the same cadence as a sermon! Perhaps Sandford doubled as a minister, she thought fancifully, and rehearsed his oration in the servants' sitting-room.

Well, that was one problem she did not have to consider!

She tapped on the door of Jonathan's study, and, on his invitation, entered. Jonathan frowned at her over his work table.

"Well," he said forcefully, "did you talk to your superior?"

Taken aback, she could only say in a faint voice, "Yes, I did. I called collect."

He waved a hand impatiently. "What did you tell him?"

She could not tell him all she had said. "Simply —" she improvised swiftly, "that I had arrived safely and that we had talked over the contract."

"You're l—" She was sure he stopped on the verge of calling her a liar, and she felt rising anger. She began to see that Jonathan could be a very nasty customer indeed, and she grasped at the vanishing shreds of her control. She could not afford to lose her temper, not until she had the contract signed.

But Jonathan underwent one of those quick changes of mood that she had seen before. Now he smiled at her — she could not help it, she thought, if she was reminded of a crocodile — and said, "And you'll be able to report a successful conclusion very soon."

Then, so smoothly that the question took her aback, he added, "Did you find out about Lewis Hyde? What did he say?"

In spite of the offhand way in which the question had been asked, she was aware of a feeling of anxious waiting in Jonathan that counseled caution on her part. She groped for an answer — what did he want? What should she say?

"You didn't even ask Danvers what his attorney thinks," Jonathan diagnosed, with contempt in his voice. It was obvious that he thought she was incapable of the task Paul had set for her. "Call him back and ask him."

"But the contract will —"

He lifted the phone and handed it to her. "Call."

Obediently she took the phone from him. Paul was even more impatient than before. "Lewis? He doesn't like it. But he'll have to go along with it. Alison, George Smith called this morning. You know what that means."

She did indeed. Cradling the phone absently, she sorted quickly through the conversation for the right words to relate to Jonathan. "Lewis doesn't like it?" Jonathan said after she had reported. He rubbed his hands together gleefully and went to the window to look out across the brown lawn under dirty, scudding clouds.

George Smith was the banker who held the financial fate of Danvers Publishing in his hands. Paul was telling her that his situation was desperate. And he counted on her to save him! Well, she would do her best.

And then she saw the envelope on Jonathan's work table. It must have come in this morning's mail. One glance was sufficient to assure her: crudely printed, with no return address, it was a duplicate of the envelope under the blotter in the library.

She looked up, suddenly aware of silence in the room. Jonathan was eying her narrowly.

"What is it?" she breathed, without caution. "What does it mean?" She pointed to the crude and therefore menacing envelope.

"Nothing," he denied too quickly.

She could not drop the matter there. "Are

you in some kind of trouble?"

She had gone too far. Through tight lips, he said quietly, "I wonder what my nephew told you."

"Does it have something to do with the book?" she demanded.

"No!" he fairly shouted.

But as she closed the door behind her and stood breathing quickly in the silent hall, she knew that Jonathan Warwick was lying.

CHAPTER FOUR

She turned away from the study door, feeling almost as though she were being pursued. And yet Jonathan had stood without moving at the window when she fled the room.

She hurried up the stairs toward her bedroom, with no clear-cut plan except escape. But as she neared the second floor, her steps slowed and she lost herself in speculation.

Fortunately the house had a simple floor plan; she had only to turn three doors to her left to find her room.

Once inside she closed the door behind her, and fleetingly wished for a sturdy bolt to draw across it. But against what? Her thoughts could not be held at bay by any bolt of iron.

Still without any sort of plan, she drew her suitcase from the closet and opened it on the bed, ready to pack. She wanted to go home — that was all there was to it. Out of this place, back to Paul.

She stopped short with her hands on the hangers. Her imagination had brought her a picture of her reception by Paul Danvers if she were to arrive in his office without the contract.

She had seen his temper on more than one occasion, but always directed at someone else. His was a cold, steely kind of anger, sparking from blue eyes that could pierce whatever armor one could put on. And he possessed a devastating sarcasm that withered what it touched.

She went back to the bed, closed the suitcase and put it back in the closet. She had better use her energy in thinking of a way to get Jonathan's signature on the right line.

She dropped into a deep armchair and then, too restless to remain long in one place, leaped to her feet and paced back and forth.

Jonathan was obviously receiving mail that distressed him. She had seen it herself, and Dan was suspicious. He had asked his uncle about it the night before. She could not be sure that it had to do with the manuscript — Jonathan's storehouse of spite — but then, suppose it did? If this was a sample of

47

what might result after the book was in print — her imagination refused to deal with that awesome concept.

Jonathan had evaded her question when she asked whether he was in trouble. If he were in trouble, what would that mean to Danvers Publishing? If he could not finish the manuscript, Paul's last chance would vanish.

A long time elapsed, and she was surprised when she glanced at her bedside clock as she stalked past it, wrapped in troubled thoughts. That long? And she had no results to show for all her troubled thoughts.

Nothing, she realized, but a full-grown and insistent doubt as to whether she really wanted to see Jonathan's book in print.

"What am I getting into?" she said aloud, and then, hearing the question, answered it with another. "What am I already up to my ears in?"

There was no answer to either question, but only an urgency to get the contract signed before that odious nephew of Jonathan's could prevent it.

She had reached the window again in her pacing, and looked idly across the frozen ground. Far in the west lay a low bank of charcoal-colored clouds, looking almost like a range of mountains in the distance. Dan's mocking words of the morning came back: "You might get snowed in — with me."

"Ha!" she said, dispelling that notion with vigor. But at the far end of the lawn, which sloped down toward the farm buildings, something in motion caught her eye. She looked more closely.

The object moved in little running spurts, and then stopped, like a frightened animal seeking to escape. But it was too large —

Something familiar about it, a certain rhythm, nudged her memory. The object was the wrong color. Now if it wore purple and green —

Snatching up her jacket, she raced out of the room and down the stairs, thrusting her arms into the sleeves on the way. At least she could clear up one of the mysteries she had discovered. She savored in advance the delicious moment when she would point out to Dan Warwick that there had indeed been something in purple that ran around the grounds.

When she burst out onto the lawn, though, she could not see the object of her search. Cautiously, she approached the verge from which the lawn sloped sharply downward to a hedge running along the bottom of the hill. Nothing stirred. The sky was gray and the light dim, but she searched the hedge bush by bush — and saw nothing.

Disappointment was sharper than she had expected. It seemed that even the shrubbery conspired to set her back. And then she saw the little twitch of movement at the far end of the row of bushes. There was someone there!

"Hey, wait!" she called. Her words had an effect opposite to her intention. It was as though a spur had been applied, for the boy — she could see him better now, and judged him to be about twelve — took to his heels like a rabbit.

She was a good runner, but he had the advantage of a head start. And of knowing where he was going.

She put on an extra burst of speed around the garage where she had found Dan that morning, then through a maze of smaller buildings that she saw only as blurs. Then she lost him.

Disgusted now, she assessed the possibility of going over the fence as a shortcut rather than following the angle of the lane. Even as she topped the fence and dropped down onto the earth, she realized that the boy had vanished.

"Drat!" she said, knowing it would not relieve her feelings. There were stronger words, but they did not immediately come to her mind.

She was answered. A low groan of sorts, accompanied by an eerie whuffle, interrupted her monologue.

She looked up into a pair of red eyes set in a long black face, attached — she felt a scream rising — to an enormous black body with four flaming hooves.

It came toward her, repeating the whuffle.

"Nice cow, nice cow," she said idiotically, trying to soothe the beast long enough to back toward the safety of the fence. Wherever it was! She reached with a hand behind her for the cold wire, but her outstretched fingers touched only air.

A step toward her, and then the animal stopped and watched her curiously.

Panic drummed in her ears, but she forced a semblance of quiet in her mind. As her vision cleared and she could examine the animal that stood in front of her, she began to feel that she could perhaps survive this encounter — if she were careful.

"Nice cow," she said again, making her tone as friendly as she could. "You're just curious, aren't you? That's all right. I expect I'm as much of a novelty to you as you are to me."

She was momentarily thankful that no one was watching this exhibition of girl and cow

51

holding a one-sided conversation, but she noticed that when she stopped talking, the animal edged closer. And when her voice broke out again, the creature stopped.

"I may have to recite the Gettysburg Address to you before we're through," she confided to the animal. "But if I can just find the fence post —*where* is it? — I'll leave you to your meditations, whatever they might be."

She talked on, stepping backward very cautiously as she did so, the words coming quickly when the beast responded with a snort that sounded unnecessarily aggressive.

At last — oh, jubilation! — her fingers touched the wire. She moved more quickly then. "Now, cow," she admonished, "just another minute and I'll be out of your hair. I hope," she added quickly, "you don't take that literally."

The rest of it was over in a flash. She turned her back on the animal and climbed over the fence, teetering precariously on top of the heavy corner post.

The black animal, curiosity still unappeased, made a little rush at the fence.

She screamed, a small frightened cry, and lost her balance. She landed in a patch of dead weeds and lost her breath. And then she heard another sound, a despicable, taunting sound.

She traced it to its source, and a red tide of anger swept over her. "How helpful you are!" She summoned up all her icy scorn and poured it over Dan Warwick, who was leaning against the side of a nearby building, laughing helplessly.

"If you could just see —" Dan tried to speak, but then surrendered again to mirth.

She reflected. It must have been funny, she conceded, even though her humiliation was still bitter. She cast a daring glance at the animal, a great heavy creature that looked at her with what she suddenly thought might be honest concern. How could she have been afraid of such a kindly beast?

She giggled reluctantly, and then the tumbling tide of laughter swept over her too.

Dan was the first to recover. "Now then," he said, in a friendlier voice than she had yet heard, "let me help you up. Are you hurt?"

She tested her arms and legs. "Nothing but my pride," she admitted.

"I didn't know you had an interest in the operation of the farm," he told her gravely, "I would have taken you on a tour."

She dismissed that. Instead she looked

searchingly at the animal who had frightened her so. "I wish it could talk," she said. "It would have saved a lot of trouble."

"They do talk, you know. Once a year." She looked swiftly at him, but he appeared to be serious. "On Christmas Eve. An old legend claims that the animals are given the gift of speech that one night, as a reward for their presence on the first Christmas."

"Really?"

"We can check up on it this year, if you like."

His eyes held a mixture of emotions that she could not analyze, but paramount among them, she thought, was mocking derision.

"I never had the — incentive, shall I say? A pretty girl, a quiet stable. Who knows what might happen?"

She had intended to tell Dan about the fleet-footed boy she had chased, but she realized ruefully that she had expected to have the boy in hand. Now there was no way to explain what she was doing here, or that she had been right about the purple-clad runner. She had no proof.

She looked up defiantly at Dan. He really was very tall. The derision in his eyes vanished. "Are you sure you're not hurt?" he said. "Your cheek —" He reached a bare fingertip to brush away the smudge. "You scratched it, probably on one of the weeds. Let's get up to the house and put something on it."

"No!" she said, too loudly.

She was reluctant to return to the house, with the shadow of Jonathan darkening it.

"What happened?" he said sharply. He suddenly seemed more as she had seen him that first night, grim, determined, and confident. Suddenly she shared that confidence. Dan would know what to do about Jonathan and his odd correspondence and his lying and the manuscript.

But she could not say a word to Dan, not in fairness to Paul. She wished Paul were there. But he was not, and Dan was.

"Nothing, really," she said untruthfully, reflecting that Jonathan had a bad effect on everyone he associated with.

Dan fell in with her as she started back to the house. He beguiled the time by pointing out various buildings — the corn crib, the barns, other that she paid no heed to. He said at last, "You're not really interested in farming, are you? You haven't heard a word I've said. I suppose I should have expected that from a girl brought up in the city."

She forced herself to respond. "Why do you stay here? You could certainly find something that suited you in the city. You have talents —" Suddenly she was aware that she sounded patronizing, even though she hadn't intended to. Her voice trailed away and they walked the rest of the way in silence.

There was no one in the kitchen when they entered. Pots on the outsize range were steaming, and one was emitting ominous scorching odors. Alison sped to the stove and turned off the burners.

She looked at Dan with surprise. "What's going on? I wouldn't think Mrs. Gibson would leave the stove unattended for that long. The pans are all dry."

She became aware of odd bumping noises from somewhere. Dan was already through the door before she could follow. He held a hand out to restrain Alison, and in an impromptu conspiracy of silence, they watched the extraordinary scene in the front hall: Mrs. Gibson, hands clutching a crumpled corner of her apron, Sandford helplessly at her side — and Jonathan, white with fury, in the door of the library. And all of them were intent upon the apparition just inside the front door.

A woman — of uncertain age, Alison thought — with too much makeup, too many jangling chains, and a bear-like fur coat, was sitting on two large suitcases. Presumably they had produced the bumping sounds.

"Jonathan," the woman said in a surprisingly sweet voice, "I plan to stay until we finish our business. To my satisfaction."

She appeared sublimely unconcerned by Jonathan's obvious rage, or the stupefaction of the others facing her. She produced a lighter and lit the cigarette dangling from her lips, in a grand display of composure.

But the hand that held the lighter, Alison noted, shook like a dead leaf in a December gale.

CHAPTER FIVE

Jonathan behaved in a way that, Alison was learning, could be described as typical. Without a word he turned his back on the scene and closed the library door behind him.

Dan was left to deal with the lady, her luggage, and her determination. Apparently it was not the first time Dan had ever been presented with a household crisis. He took over with practiced competence.

Crossing the tiled floor to greet the uninvited guest with at least an appearance of cordiality, he introduced himself.

"Mr. Warwick's nephew," he clarified. "And you are?"

"Mrs. Rice," she told him. "Eugenia Rice. And I'm sorry for you if you're related to *him*." She nodded her head vigorously toward the library door.

Mrs. Gibson was muttering in Alison's ear. "What does she mean, to stay in the hall? If she expects the old man to kowtow to her, she'll be here forever. It's all the fault of that terrible book!"

Alison could only agree.

Whatever Eugenia had said next to Dan was lost to Alison because of the cook's outburst, but it seemed effective. Dan turned to the others and, with a quelling look, gave directions that Eugenia's bags were to be taken upstairs; there would be one additional guest at lunch.

But there was more to come. Just before lunch, Alison stepped out onto the broad front porch. The house was kept hothouse warm, and she began to feel she could not breathe in it. But perhaps it was more than the furnace running riot.

She had tried to call Paul again. Jonathan had been most insistent that Lewis Hyde come down to discuss the contract. And he had insisted that he would sign nothing until that happened. But Paul was not in his office, and his secretary claimed not to know where he was.

So, on the front porch, Alison had a full view of what happened next. The sky seemed even more leaden and gloomy than it had before. Dan had said a storm was brewing. Alison was used to hearing predictions on the radio, but here she realized she could actually watch the storm as it came. In the city, with only a patch of blue or gray showing between buildings, the sky meant little. Here it was a large share of the environment.

The gray bank in the west, which had looked, a couple of hours ago, like a distant mountain range, had now risen to fill a quarter of the sky. The storm's forerunners, dirty gray wisps with shredded edges, raced across the sky, nearly low enough to touch with an outstretched hand. A chill wind gusted fitfully around the corners of the house.

The wind's roar was almost loud enough in her ears to muffle the sound of a racing motor approaching at considerable speed. Another unexpected visitor at Jonathan Warwick's house? Well, she thought wryly, more like Eugenia Rice, they didn't need.

The motor roar suddenly broke in the middle and seemed to shatter, and then all was quiet. Something had happened. She ran down the steps and across the broad turnaround, and then hesitated. She should probably call for help. But she had better find out what help was needed, if any. It might have been a car on the outside road, she told herself.

She ran down the driveway to the first

turn. There it was — a small foreign car, tilted up on the verge of the driveway, nosed against a mammoth tree. The car must have taken the brunt of the impact, and yet it had stood up well against the crash. The driver was just now climbing out.

"What happened?" she cried, still at a distance.

The driver turned and looked at her with dislike. His mammoth sungoggles might have been fashionable, but they must have reduced his vision considerably.

"Couldn't you make the turn?"

Words trembled on his lips, but he held them back. He was a small man, hardly taller than Alison, and reed-thin. She almost expected him to sway in the breeze.

"That was pretty silly," she confessed, with an effort at friendliness. She didn't like this man very much, even though he hadn't said a word yet. "I can see you couldn't."

"I skidded," hc said, pointing out the obvious. "What's this road made of, anyway — glass?"

"Only the frost on the blacktop," she said with assurance, as if she had been born knowing it. "Would you like to come up to the house? There's a phone, of course."

"Your house?" he asked in apprehension.

"No, Mr. Warwick's house. But I'm sure —"

There was just a slight relaxation in the stiff figure before her. Suddenly she realized she hadn't even asked him if he was injured.

"No," he said shortly in response to her belated inquiry, but then — she wished he would take off those idiotic goggles — she could not see into his eyes. She guessed that they hid a sudden wariness, because he changed his mind. "Yes, a bit," he said, and tested his right ankle. "I think it's sprained."

He hadn't limped at first, she noticed, and then told herself that the shock had worn off now and probably the pain had begun.

He took a small case from the back of the car. "Don't like to leave valuables in the open, you know," he said. But she thought uneasily that it looked as if he were prepared to spend a weekend.

So there were four for lunch that day before the storm hit — Dan, Alison, Eugenia, and the newcomer. "Call me Ferdy," was the only information he allowed to escape him.

"A mystery man," Dan said, not very originally. "Where did he come from?"

"I'm sorry," she said. "The front license plate is mixed up with the tree bark, and I didn't feel I wanted to trot around to the back of the car. Besides, I had no idea I would be called on to provide the information."

"Don't get huffy," he said. "It doesn't suit you."

"What *does* suit me?" she asked without thinking, and then too late perceived the trap. "Never mind. I don't want to know."

"We can look at the car when we go to town."

"We?" she echoed blankly. "Town?"

"You'll need a coat, but I think we'll be home before the weather turns nasty."

When she stood later in the front hall, her heavy jacket buttoned up to her chin and her woolen scarf in her hand, she noticed that Jonathan still lurked behind the closed door of the library. That was one way to avoid an unwanted guest, she thought with amusement, and wondered how long it would take before Eugenia found she hadn't a chance against the wily author.

She heard voices from the library, and she was suddenly transported back to her arrival the day before. This time, however, it was not Dan shouting at Jonathan Warwick. She listened in spite of herself, straining to hear through the closed door.

Had Eugenia finally managed to get to Jonathan?

A slight noise behind her startled her and she turned to see Eugenia standing in the doorway of the dining room.

Eugenia too was listening. Alison had got as far as framing a pertinent question when the sound of a horn at the front door reminded her that Dan was waiting. With a word of excuse, she left Eugenia to eavesdrop on the vociferous discussion in the library, and ran out to climb into the large station wagon.

Down the driveway, Dan pulled to a halt beside the abandoned car of their mystery guest. She watched him inspect the license plate on the back, and he spent quite a long time examining the damage to the front. He said nothing as he climbed back into the wagon. She was at the point of asking him something, anything, but he forestalled her.

"Today is a day to spend far, far away from the wicked memories of an old man," Dan told her. "You're a city girl, you tell me. I want you to learn about the country."

Curiosity stirred in her, but it took an unexpected turn. "Why should I?"

He glanced at her in surprise. "Why, you'll have to know it before you can say you like it, won't you?"

"But I'm not going to like it," she said stubbornly.

Crockett was perhaps six miles away from the Warwick house. Dan knew everybody, or so it seemed. She tagged along behind him, sometimes running to catch up, while they bought supplies.

When they got back to the station wagon and she saw that even a full roll of fencing had been fitted in, in addition to a phenomenal amount of groceries, she wondered aloud what could be left for the inhabitants of Crockett to buy during the next week.

"This is a little more than usual," he admitted, "but the storm may last a week. And with an influx of unexpected guests —"

"A week?" she echoed with dismay. "Do you mean that we could be snowed in for a *week?*"

"At least," he said serenely. "You remember I mentioned it to you earlier. It will be great fun."

She closed her eyes and felt her high spirits oozing away. A week with Dan? And Eugenia, and Jonathan, and even Ferdy?

"If we hurry," she insisted, "we can get back and I can be on my way home."

"Right into the teeth of the storm," he pointed out. "You would be going west? Look."

His finger indicated the ominous gray

65

bank, now nearly at the zenith. How fast it had risen! And even as she looked at it, the first snowflakes danced through the air.

"I give up," she said softly.

He looked down at her with approval. "You're less nervous already," he said. "That's a good sign."

This time she was too wary to fall into whatever trap he had laid for her — a good sign of what? She longed to know, but was determined not to ask.

They did not go directly back to the War-wick house. It almost seemed as if Dan were reluctant to return, and, on consideration, she agreed. Back at the Warwick house there was stress to spare.

He drove around the town in apparent aimlessness, pointing out lawns and houses where the Christmas decorations were already lit against the coming darkness.

"There's a prize for the best," he told her.

"How could you decide?" she marveled. She looked sideways at him, noticing for the first time the strong line of his jaw and the long crease from cheek to mouth that softened his harsh profile. Far too rugged for her taste, she decided, recalling Paul's perfect features.

She turned quickly away. They were pass-ing a charming brick church with a white steeple, in New England style. She wondered idly if they would have a Christmas service — and then realized that if they were snowed in, she couldn't make it anyway.

"No Christmas service," he said, answering her question, "but there will be a Christmas Eve pageant."

At last he turned the car in the direction of home. The snow was coming faster now and the pavement glistened with moisture. The thick white flakes endlessly hurled themselves into the headlights, and the monotony, together with the heat pouring out at her feet, made her remarkably sleepy. She shook herself to wakefulness. If she talked, she could stay alert.

The one thing that had teased her all afternoon sprang to her lips. "What do you suppose Ferdy could have to say to your uncle?"

The car swerved. "Ferdy? Uncle Jonathan?"

She told him then of hearing the raised voices from the library, and of thinking that it was Eugenia arguing with him again. But the woman had been behind her in the doorway.

"And now that I think about it," Alison concluded, "that woman looked scared. Dan," she added, twisting in her seat to look at him, "what's going on? Why does Eugenia insist on seeing Jonathan? Why won't he talk to her? And why is she so frightened? Did you see her hand shake this morning?"

She had no doubt of his attention. It was riveted on her, evidenced by his slowing the car to a crawl.

"Go on."

"And who is Ferdy? Dan, do you suppose it's all over this dumb manuscript?"

"The one that you insist on publishing?" Dan pointed out coldly.

"The one I have been instructed to buy," she corrected him, trying to match his aloofness. She cast to the winds her own part in convincing Paul, and then the executive board, to accept the manuscript.

"That book —" Dan mused, as though she were not present at all, "there's something he's got in mind, and I don't know what it is. . . . Yet."

"To get the book published?" she offered.

He didn't answer. Instead, he posed another question.

"Why do you suppose Ferdy's car is not damaged at all?"

"What?"

"He only pushed the car, very gently, into the tree. In fact, the accident was a phony."

"But he said he was hurt!" she remembered.

"The accident was phony," Dan repeated firmly, "and so, I strongly suspect, is Ferdy."

CHAPTER SIX

Alison lapsed into silence. There was so much to think about, and none of her thoughts brought comfort. The manuscript, at first impressing her as being witty, had lost its light touch now that she had met Jonathan and seen the malice etched in his face, and flashing from his eyes.

But she was committed to the book now, propelled by Paul's great need of a best-selling product, and the direct orders of the executive board of Danvers Publishing — the instructions she had worked so hard to obtain. Now she wished she had never heard of Jonathan Warwick, or his book.

The windshield wipers were working now, and their monotonous whoosh kept time to the repetitive thoughts going around and around in her brain. Jonathan, the book, Ferdy, Eugenia.

She sighed hugely and reached out a gloved hand to wipe away the condensation on the car window. Peering out into the gathering darkness, she could not suppress a shudder.

"Nothing dangerous out there," her companion said. "Not as dangerous as a city street, from what I read."

"How did you know what I was thinking?" she demanded.

His only answer was a smile.

She realized then that they were traveling at a much slower speed than before. The wipers were sweeping fast, and yet the snow piled up at either end of their semicircular track. The wind had risen, too, and she could feel the gusts against the side of the station wagon.

Loaded as it was, she wondered whether the wagon was more vulnerable to wind, or would have an added stability. In answer to her question Dan said, "I just hope we get home all right. I'd hate to walk five miles in this."

She huddled into her jacket, turning the collar up around her throat. The hazards of country living were far worse than she had imagined.

"I didn't mean to frighten you," he said suddenly. "We will make it all right. But with this wind, if it starts drifting —"

At that moment the road dipped into a

hollow; already the snow was beginning to pile up. Another hour, she thought, might find the hollow so deep in drift that the road would be impassable.

"Now I understand all the groceries," she said abruptly, the full significance of the storm breaking over her.

"Snowed in," Dan pointed out, "as I said."

"I should have gone then," she argued, but even as she spoke she knew the storm had come up too fast.

It was then that she became aware that they were being followed. Followed? Surely it was just another car on the same road behind them, she thought, and yet when Dan slowed, on a wider stretch of road, the car dropped back and refused to take advantage of the opportunity.

"Dan?" she said softly.

"I see them," he answered. "Probably one of the neighbors, not taking any chances."

"Not that I'm uneasy or anything," she pointed out, "but I've got a bad case of jittery nerves."

"All right," he said, and then slowed to a crawl. "They've got to go past now."

But they didn't. The car hung well back, almost stopping. Dan muttered something under his breath and started up again. "Nothing to hide," he said with a touch of ferocity. "We're imagining things, that's all."

How warming it was to hear him say "we," as if he too were worried. The storm worsened by the minute, and soon she realized that Dan needed all his concentration for driving. She took up the watch, noting the regular progress of the car that followed them, now at such a distance that she could see only the headlights, and not any details of the car.

"Now why," Dan said as if to himself, "would you think there was something frightening about being followed?"

She had been lulled into a friendly kind of tolerance on this expedition to town, she realized, but now that they were nearly home again, she would have to regard Dan as her enemy, at least as far as the book was concerned. She wished that she could trust him, but her loyalty was centered on Paul, and she was content with that.

"What do you know that I don't know?" he continued, still in that wondering voice.

She had to answer him. "Nothing," she said, more tartness in her voice than she expected. "You know about the letters."

"Letters?" he said quickly. "Tell me what you know. It's important, Alison."

She told him about the letter that had crept out from under the blotter in

Jonathan's library, and the one on his work table in the study. She sighed in vast relief. "I don't know why they bothered me so much," she confessed. "Probably nothing to it, but somehow, they were frightening."

He took one hand from the wheel to touch her sleeve briefly. "I don't know what's in the letters," he told her soberly, "but I don't like the look of things." After a long time, punctuated only by the sound of the wipers and the buffeting of the wind. he added, "The thing is — and I'm sure you see it too — Uncle Jonathan is frightened. That's what worries me."

It seemed hours before they had traversed the six miles to the gates of Jonathan Warwick's house. Dan negotiated the turn carefully, feeling the wheels slip once, and then again, but at last they caught and he drew the car to a halt.

"Stay here," he commanded, as he left the car and walked to the rear. The car behind them had turned into the driveway too. Probably a stranger, she thought, following the only car on the road, hoping for directions. Dan was gone for some minutes, and when he returned his face was set in stern lines.

"Did you see any name like Sawyer in that manuscript?" he asked her.

Surprised into silence, she turned over in her mind the chapters she had seen. "N— no," she said at last. "I don't think so. Why?"

"That man behind us," he explained. "Said he was lost, and asked for directions. I told him where he was, and I'm positive he recognized the name." He thought for a minute, and then added, "Almost positive. He did ask for the Reeds, half a mile down the road."

"Suppose he did come to see your uncle. Couldn't he have something to do with your uncle's farm? Like a —" she cast about wildly, "a livestock buyer? or a seed salesman?"

"Not likely." He smiled, as if amused by a private thought.

After he had set the car in motion again, he said, "How much of the book have you read?"

"Five chapters," she answered promptly. "It's the rest of the book that promises to be so — controversial, I guess you would say."

"Then he hasn't really injured anybody yet?"

"No, not really. A good many sly digs, you know. But nothing — dangerous." As soon as she had spoken, she wondered why that particular word had leapt to her lips.

By the time they had reached the turn-around there was no more time to speculate. Dan offered to let her out there, but she said, "I'll go with you to put the car away."

They pulled up to the back of the great house, and Sandford ran down the steps to help unload the station wagon. He said a few words in a low tone to Dan, but Alison could not hear them. Dan threw his head up sharply. Apparently he didn't like what he had been told. He turned to her and said roughly, "Apparently we've been invaded." He refused to answer her questions, saying only, "Run along inside. We want to get the supplies unloaded as fast as we can."

She pulled herself up the steps to the door. Suddenly she was tired, even in her bones. A long, hot bath was what she needed. And silence, lots of it. She was weary of people, of all the unanswered, perhaps unanswerable, questions.

Solitude — that was what she wanted.

Across her thoughts came a high-pitched voice, one that rose and fell, saying outlandish things. "Lo! what light breaks in yonder sky?" There was something wrong with that quotation, she thought, but could not quite pin it down. Drawn as if by a magnet, she moved toward the source of the voice.

Down the hall, the kitchen door stood half

open; she pushed the door wide. Mrs. Gibson was at the stove. Steam rose from the pots and a comforting burble sounded in the great percolator. A scent of cinnamon, mixed with bay leaf, coffee, and apples filled the room.

And in the center of the room, arms outstrteched to the ceiling, face blank with astonishment at the sight of her, stood a boy of perhaps twelve. He wore a green turban on his head.

"What on earth —" she breathed.

Mrs. Gibson crossed the room swiftly. "My grandson Jerry, Miss Monroe."

Jerry recovered sufficiently to mutter a quick, "Hi," and turned to flee.

"Jerry," Alison said insistently. "Do you — this seems a silly question — does that turban go with something purple?"

"You saw me," he said, accusingly. "Gramma said you couldn't have, but I knew all the time you did."

"Yes, I did. Nearly wrecked the car." To say nothing of earning Dan's derision. Suddenly she was suspicious. "Dan kept me talking long enough for you to get out of the way, didn't he?"

"I didn't want to wear that dumb stuff," he burst out bitterly. "But we had a rehearsal, and Mrs. Bond dropped me off at the gate, and I had to come up the road in that dumb purple thing. Wise Man, ha! In that dumb hat?"

"Rehearsal?" It was Alison's turn to echo blankly.

"For the pageant," he said impatiently.

"At the church," Mrs. Gibson added. "Now Jerry, run along and help Sandford and Dan."

"The church in Crockett has a Christmas Eve program," she continued. "And the Sunday School has a part in it. It's so hard to get kids to do anything." She looked darkly after Jerry.

"That's only three days away," Alison observed. "With this snow, I wonder if you can get to town."

"If I didn't know that Providence had its own ways, I would suspect young Jerry of praying for this blizzard."

Alison was amused. "Maybe he did, and Providence is on his side."

Mrs. Gibson flashed her an understanding look. "Did you really see him out there? You look done in. Let me pour you some coffee."

They sat together at the wooden table, so scrubbed it was nearly white. Alison related the incident of "the purple running thing."

"That Dan!" Mrs. Gibson laughed. Then

in a more sober mood, she said, "You could do a lot worse."

"I don't know what you mean."

"You'll come to it. And," she swiftly changed the subject, "where's that Emmalu?"

Emmalu was the girl who had unpacked Alison's bag when she arrived, the invisible genie who furnished fresh towels, made beds, and, apparently, helped in the kitchen.

Alison lingered over her coffee. The kitchen was very warm, and the homey smells and sounds were comforting to her. She was reluctant to stir herself enough to go upstairs to dress for dinner.

So she was still there when Emmalu entered with a gust of fresh cold air and a spattering of snowflakes on her blonde hair. Breathlessly, she cried, "It's terrible out there!"

"Never mind," Mrs. Gibson told her tartly. "It's a regular dinner party we're having tonight, what with all the extra people that arrived out of the storm, and if you ask me, which nobody has nor will, some of them aren't all they say they are."

Alison perceived that she was in the way, so she took her cup and saucer to the sink and rinsed the cup out before setting it on the drainboard. She caught a flash of approval in Mrs. Gibson's eye, and was unreasonably pleased.

Leaving the kitchen behind her, she emerged into the front hall, brightly lit and cooler than the kitchen. She thought how accustomed she was getting to the house; it was as familiar as though she had lived there for weeks, instead of having just arrived twenty-four hours before.

She was aware of voices from the living room, across the hall from the library. Thank goodness they sounded friendly! She had had enough of voices raised in argument. She wondered idly where Eugenia was. Perhaps she had left after all.

But there were other voices, and suddenly one — she could hardly believe her ears! — close to the living room door. The owner of it stepped into the hall, and she looked full into his face.

"Paul!" she cried. "You didn't tell me you were coming down! How marvelous to see you!"

It was surprising how much effort she had to make to sound welcoming. She must be wearier than she thought.

"Well, Alison," he said, an unaccustomed glint in his eyes. "You didn't seem to be able to get the old man to sign, so something had to be done."

She was moving toward him, expecting his kiss, but the note in his voice held her off. "That's not fair!" she retorted. "I've been here less than a day."

"Time enough," he said, but he did not meet her eyes. Something had gone very wrong here, she realized, but she could not guess what it was.

"Paul, I tried to call you back," she began to explain, but she heard a submissive note in her voice that she deplored. Well, she would wait and see what had gone wrong, wait till he asked her for explanations, wait —

Angry and hurt, she brushed past him to the stairway. "Too bad you made the trip for nothing," she said coolly, "and of course now you're marooned here. You'll never make it back to town in this storm."

She began to climb the stairs. She would not look back at Paul, lest he see the disappointment in her eyes. But when a new voice spoke behind her, she whirled in sheer astonishment, nearly losing her grip on the banister.

She knew that sleek, exquisite woman who stood with one hand possessively linked through Paul's arm, looking up at him with a gleam of satisfaction.

"Snowbound?" said Sandra Hyde. "With you, Paul? What fun!"

CHAPTER SEVEN

Already the entire house wore a Christmas air. The banisters were entwined with ropes of gold and silver tinsel, the newel held a mammoth urn of holly, a ball of mistletoe hung from the hall ceiling, and the scent of pine climbed up the stairs with Alison.

But her mind was far from holiday festivities. As she stepped into her bedroom and closed the door behind her like a rabbit scuttling into the brush, she felt like Ebenezer Scrooge.

As unheeding as a sleepwalker, she crossed to the window and sank down on the padded window seat. The glass was cold to her forehead, and at length soothed her feverish thoughts. The wind blew snow in a wildly flapping curtain of white, and in spite of herself she shivered. Out there the elements were fierce and deadly. Inside the sturdy brick walls of the house emotions were gathering as fierce as the blizzard.

And her own were as unruly as anyone's.

First of all, Paul Danvers himself was downstairs. Had he come to help her through the business of her first contract? Somehow, remembering his impatiently critical words to her in the hall, she couldn't gather much reassurance from his presence.

And Sandra Hyde was here. Certainly she had nothing to do with Jonathan and his contract. Had she come along to keep an eye on Paul? Little things came back to Alison now as the quiet of the room put some kind of order into her churning thoughts — little things previously unnoticed that now reinforced Alison's new-found suspicion that Sandra had more than a passing interest in Paul's life.

Now that she thought about it, she recognized one of the other voices in the living room downstairs — Sandra's father.

Paul, Sandra, Lewis — all descending here to take the negotiations with Jonathan out of her hands. Admit it, Alison, she advised herself — your first big chance, and Paul doesn't trust you.

She tasted disappointment and defeat. Well, Dan Warwick has a lot to answer for, she thought darkly. If he had minded his own business, she could have dealt easily with his uncle, she was sure.

Jonathan, who had started the whole thing with his foolish, infantile lashing of dead horses of his past. It was strange, she thought in passing, how her ideas had changed. Only a week ago, this manuscript promised to be a wonderfully witty book. Now —

She sat long at the window, feeling too weary to move. If only she could stay here forever, she thought, until the snow covered the window sill, freezing her where she sat. Then she would not have to go downstairs and see Paul and Sandra — snowed in together, as Sandra had gleefully pointed out.

A tap at the door roused her. Emmalu scurried in, carrying an armful of towels. "Shall I run your bath, Miss Monroe?"

"No, Emmalu, I'll do that. You've got your hands full, no doubt."

"Oh, you wouldn't believe!" Emmalu cried. "Towels for all the rooms, and I'm to help serve at dinner, and Jenny Pitman can't get here to help in the kitchen — although what help she'd be anyway I don't know, I'm sure — and my cap won't stay on, and I don't know what all!"

The tirade ended in a heartfelt wail, and the girl was gone before Alison could sympathize.

Alison smiled. She hadn't thought what the influx of — she counted on her fingers — five new guests might mean to the staff. The population had exploded. Overnight. She wished with all her heart that she was back in her tiny apartment, even though the west wind would be rattling the ill-fitting windows, puffing out the draperies.

The Christmas decorations must have taken all day to put up, she realized as she came down to dinner. The living room displayed great heaps of pine dangled over the door like a Victorian drapery.

The living room seemed full of people. She moved through, speaking to them all. Sandra was dressed in an ivory creation that set off her red hair — and her figure — in a spectacular fashion. Alison hardly noticed the dress, only Sandra's expression; it made Alison think of a cat waiting at a mouse-hole.

Lewis Hyde was tall, courtly, and elegant in his dinner jacket. His white hair and thin, monk-like face gave the impression of cynical wisdom, as though he had looked on the world's foibles and generously decided to accept them.

Paul, of course, was as handsome as an illustration in a magazine, but full of nervous energy that made him look unsettled, marring the perfection of his profile.

Ferdy — who was he, anyway? — wore a vague expression on his face and carried on an even vaguer conversation. If anyone could be in a room and still be invisible, Ferdy was that man.

As for Eugenia, her light brown hair was fluffed up unprofessionally, and her brown lace dress looked even tackier in contrast to Sandra's impeccable grooming.

Dan put a glass of sherry in Alison's hand, murmuring in an undertone, "The wolves are gathering." She looked inquiringly at him, but he had turned away, gazing at Sandra with obvious admiration. In a moment he had moved toward her, giving the impression that he was being drawn by a magnet, against his will. Alison thought that it would be a great relief if she could only stamp her foot.

Dinner was announced at the very moment Jonathan appeared in the doorway. The service at dinner was still under the direction of Sandford, but it was apparent that his assistant did not fulfill expectations. Emmalu, in a neat black uniform with a ruffled white apron, handed dishes around.

Finally Alison understood one of the remarks she had made upstairs. Emmalu's cap certainly wouldn't stay on. It careened to her left, entirely out of control. And Emmalu did not have a spare hand to take care of it.

She breathed noisily in Alison's ear as she extended a dish of asparagus. Alison was sure she could hear the muttered words, "Serve from the left." Poor Emmalu! She too longed to be somewhere else — anywhere else.

Alison looked down the table. Dan was being very kind to Eugenia, listening carefully, his dark head bent in attention. Paul was lost in his own thoughts. Sandra, next to him, leaned toward him and touched his shoulder with hers, with unnecessary frequency, Alison thought. Yet she intercepted several glances toward Dan, who returned at least one.

She could not help but compare the two men. She loved Paul — she had since the first day she had gone to work at Danvers Publishing. All this business of the manuscript was, after all, for him, for the survival of Danvers Publishing. She wished she didn't feel so confused about the book.

Jonathan had dismissed a tentative query about the manuscript with a crisp "Later. I do not discuss business at my table." Dan raised his head at that, but she could not read the expression on his face.

At long last the dinner was over and Jonathan rose. "We do not follow the practice of remaining after the ladies have left. We have too few guests to let any of them languish for a moment."

It was a courtly speech, but, as with everything Jonathan said, it carried a suggestion that if you knew him a bit better, you would hear another meaning beneath his words.

In the general rising and moving from the dining room, Sandra linked her arm possessively through Paul's and they went through the door together. Lewis followed, bowing to Ferdy as he let the little man precede him.

Alison looked up to find Dan watching her with what she suspected was pity. Suddenly his face blurred and the sting of unshed tears drove her, nearly running, into the hall. She could not face the others, not until she had seized control of herself again.

Instead of turning to the right, toward the bright chatter that drifted into the hall, she turned left into the service wing.

Leaning against the wall in the dim light, she winked furiously to hold back hot tears. At last she decided she could not stay there forever, but, equally, she could not return to the other guests.

Pushing open the swinging door to the kitchen, she blinked in the sudden bright light. Mrs. Gibson looked far wearier than she had in the afternoon. Young Jerry struggled manfully with a great stack of pans in the sink, scrubbing wildly. He looked around and caught sight of Alison. Astonishment held him captive, his tongue still protruding from a corner of his mouth as evidence of his unaccustomed labors.

Impulsively, Alison moved into the kitchen. "Mrs. Gibson, sit down at the table and finish your dinner. Where's an apron? I can't manage the dish-washer, but I know how to scrub pans. Move over, Jerry."

The atmosphere in the kitchen changed subtly. Jerry moved over instantly. Mrs. Gibson murmured, "You shouldn't, Miss Monroe." But in silent acceptance, she handed her a freshly starched apron from a drawer.

It was an endless task, she thought, one hour and three broken fingernails later. But she would not have exchanged her position there, swathed in a mammoth coverall, starched so heavily it felt like armor, up to the elbows in hot soapy water, for the company of that uneasy group.

The pageant script, produced from the depths of Emmalu's knitting bag, was now propped between the faucets above the sink, where Alison could see it easily.

Voices rose behind her, Emmalu — "As bright as yonder sky is, my lord — what comes next, Miss Monroe?"

Jerry's scornful voice broke in. "Can't you remember anything?"

"I remembered to serve from the left and take away from the right, didn't I?"

"Your cap fell off, though."

"You sound like brother and sister," Alison pointed out crisply. "You don't know your lines any better than she does, Jerry."

"They are brother and sister," Mrs. Gibson sighed.

Emmalu took up the script again. "I think this is all pretty useless. We'll never get to do it."

"Don't count on that," warned Mrs. Gibson. "You know Dan. He'll think of something."

It was surprising to Alison to see the total devotion showered on Dan. Certainly she hadn't seen anything to worship in the man. He was subject to inappropriate mirth and sudden rages. She knew that much from her own experience and from watching him talk to his uncle.

"Miss Monroe, have I got it right?"

Alison was jerked back to the present. She had to admit she hadn't heard Jerry's

91

declaimed lines. "Try again," she said. "Let's do it from the beginning. I'll read Kaspar's part."

They all bent lustily to their tasks, nearly shouting to overcome the guttural churning of the dish-washer.

"The light in yonder sky . . ." Emmalu caroled.

"We must follow, follow, follow the gleam. . . ." Jerry loudly admonished everyone within ear-shot, which could include, Alison thought darkly, even the guests taking their ease in the living room.

"There's something very familiar about some of these words," she said thoughtfully, after a stumbling run-through.

"That's because Jenny wrote it," Emmalu explained. "Jenny does all our pageants."

"Copies them," Mrs. Gibson said in disapproving tones. "A little here, a little there."

Alison nodded wisely. A little Shakespeare, a little revival hymn. But with surprise she realized that the words weren't important. It was the participation, the hard work, the discipline required in learning the words, in giving themselves whole-heartedly to the Christmas season, that made the ancient story new again. Even the wearing of "the dumb purple thing" had virtue in it. But she was too wise to try to tell that to Jerry.

"Well, Jenny knows a good thing when she copies it, I guess," Alison said. "Let's do it again. Jerry, try to remember that you're a Wise Man, and don't mumble."

When Dan came silently into the kitchen, they were in full cry. Even Mrs. Gibson lifted her bifocals so she could read through the bottom part, and exhibited an unsuspected gift for dialect as she read lines originally spoken by Hotspur but now attributed to Melchior from the East.

Herod, as portrayed by Sandford, gestured wildly as the Kings laid their knowledge before him, and Alison was enjoying herself hugely.

As the actors one by one became aware of Dan standing in the doorway, their voices died away, and suddenly everyone seemed to recall neglected, but extremely urgent, business in another part of the house.

And Alison was left alone with Dan.

She looked past him but there was no escape. He filled the doorway. Then she thought, I haven't done anything wrong, and I'm not going to be intimidated.

"The pageant," she said. "They need the practice."

"So I see."

"They — they're doing very well. Too bad the snow will cancel the program."

"Not the snow," Dan said pleasantly. "But probably a murder or two. That would put a real damper on things."

She could only stare at him.

"Especially at the season of brotherly love and goodwill," he offered in explanation.

"What are you talking about?"

"Remember the car that followed us from Crockett?"

She caught hold of the memory and added a name to it. "Sawyer, didn't you say?"

"Right. Colonel Sawyer, if you please. Just arrived out of the storm, seeking sanctuary. He couldn't make it to his destination. But I'm willing to swear Uncle Jonathan knows him!"

She could only gape at him.

"You and your manuscript," he continued. Now there was a wry bitterness in him. "You've set the cat among the pigeons, stirred up a hornet's nest — all the tried but very true phrases."

She was angry on the instant. "Don't talk to me that way. It's your uncle who wrote the book. And, by the way, I don't suppose that you ever heard of the word gratitude?"

"Gratitude. A simple word meaning to appreciate your uncle's generosity in letting you live here with him in his house, idling your time away on little errands."

She had gone too far, but it was too late to take back anything. She simply would have to put on the protective covering of haughtiness and sweep out the door.

She headed directly toward him, expecting him to step aside. In a way he did. She could not keep herself from glancing up at him as she reached the door. She had expected fury in his eyes, stoked to a blaze by her uncalled-for words, but instead — she could not be sure, but it looked very much as though he were on the verge of succumbing to his usual ill-timed amusement!

She gasped in surprise and exasperation.

His long arm reached out to bar her way. "Look up there," he said gently, and she obeyed. A ball of mistletoe swayed slightly from the top of the door frame.

"Never let anything go to waste, is my motto," he told her, and kissed her, gently at first, then with urgency. At last he released her.

Now she was positive there *was* anger in his eyes.

"You've brought nothing but trouble to this house. Go on back to your boss!" he said roughly. "You deserve each other."

CHAPTER EIGHT

He pivoted on his heel and left. She did not know how long she stood there, feeling his kiss still hard on her lips, his arms holding her. Slowly, she began to think again, and her mind skidded past the hurtful things he had said, and completely ignored the scalding retorts she had thrown at him. Instead she fixed upon the announcement that still another refugee from the storm had arrived.

Refugee? No, Dan believed that the new arrival was no chance wayfarer.

She went into the front hall. It was empty, but she heard voices from the living room. She started forward to join them, but remembered in time that she was still enveloped in the white coverall that Mrs. Gibson had lent her. She looked down ruefully at the wet spot where the sudsy water had splashed from the sink.

She removed the coverall, folded it carefully, and laid it on a chair that stood against the white paneling beneath the staircase. Just then she heard angry voices from the study behind the library.

Jonathan's, of course, but the new voice was one she did not know — the new arrival's, no doubt. She did not mean to eavesdrop, but after the first words, she was riveted to the spot.

"That whole story was a lie!"

"Colonel —" That was Jonathan, sounding surprisingly calm.

"You listen to me! That story was merely rumor, and you had better get ready for the biggest law-suit you ever saw!"

The voices fell then, so that Alison could not hear the words, but there was no question in her mind that the enraged visitor was referring to the manuscript. She recognized then what had been lying in wait in her mind until a time when she could deal with it. Now conviction came full-blown: Jonathan Warwick's manuscript was the thorniest hot potato she had ever known. She paused, thinking over that image, and then, shrugging accuracy aside, decided that "thorny hot potato" had a truth of its own.

But she must join the others in the living room. She wondered whether the angry voices could have reached that far, and decided they could not. She was only halfway to the living room when she heard Jonathan's words, now startlingly clear in the hall. "There's a strong lock on this drawer," he said, "and if it's forced, I'll know who is responsible."

They were emerging from Jonathan's white-walled study, and she ran the last few steps in order not to be found in the hall. She discovered all the others in the living room — all but Dan. He had not returned.

Lewis Hyde stood at the fireplace; one long arm was draped negligently along the mantel. The leaping fire apparently claimed his attention, for he stared broodingly into it.

Eugenia was slumped in a flowered chintz chair, oblivious of her surroundings. The heavy rouge on her cheeks and the distracted application of face powder, resulting in floury splotches, could not hide the naked misery in her eyes.

Paul and Sandra had dealt out a hand of gin rummy, and their heads were together over their game.

Alison suddenly was swept by loneliness. She might as well not exist, for all the attention she had created when she came into the room. Paul didn't even lift his head, but suddenly, as though he had read her thoughts, he moved slightly so that he could look at her out of the corner of his eye. It was a furtive look, but Sandra caught it.

She looked up, crying, "Alison! Where have you been? You missed the most astonishing thing — a snow man! He walked right into the house!"

Her father looked at her with distaste. "The storm is fierce. Listen to the wind at the shutters. The poor man had walked miles in the blizzard."

"Miles?" Surprisingly, it was Eugenia who spoke. "Hardly as far as that." She looked wildly at each of them. "Didn't he have a car?" Her agitation silenced them all. "A car," she insisted, "so we can get away from here!"

Alison was beside her at once. "Now, Mrs. Rice," she soothed, "the storm is so bad, you couldn't go anywhere now. Not until morning." She was not at all sure about morning, either, but they would deal with that in due time.

To her surprise Ferdy said, "Why not trot upstairs? A rest will do you good." Alison had not noticed Ferdy before. He was easily the most anonymous man she had ever met. "And tomorrow we can have a little talk." The suggestion, delivered in an undertone, was obviously meant for Eugenia alone.

Eugenia nodded, and tottered out of the

room. She shook off Alison's helping hand, saying "I'm all right. I'll lie down a bit." Mumbling apologies, she started up the stairs, and Alison turned back to the living room.

Eugenia's departure had released them all, as if by magic. Paul chose this moment to face Ferdy. "What are you doing here? Trying to steal Jonathan Warwick right out from under my nose?"

Ferdy hastily put a small table between Paul and himself but Paul stalked him. "Let me warn you, Ferdy — Danvers has Warwick signed up right now. You're too late."

Alison cried, "What are you talking about, Paul?"

"Don't you know this man? Let me introduce you. Ferdy Sessions of Sessions Publishing. The house that publishes all those exposé books."

"Watch what you say," Ferdy warned, with a swift glance at Lewis Hyde. "I've got witnesses."

Paul stopped. "Just remember," he finished lamely, "I've got the contract signed."

Ferdy glanced at Alison. "Is that true?"

Lewis intervened. Still lounging elegantly against the mantel, he said in his crisp, dry manner, "Don't worry. Danvers is not going to publish Jonathan Warwick."

Paul stopped as if struck. "Not publish? Not publish! Lewis, you know better than that. We've *got* to publish it!"

In a low voice, Sandra warned, "Paul."

Alison suddenly saw it all. The manuscript was not good. She had not found the year's runaway best-seller. Only the shocking revelations that might lie in the rest of the manuscript would sell that book. And, balanced against that —

Well, what could you balance against that? Eugenia Rice's misery? The rage of the unknown Colonel?

The disapproval of Dan Warwick?

Strangely, it was the last that bothered her the most. That just showed, she told herself, how upside-down everything was in this strange place. Right back to the very first night, with purple running creatures. That had been explained, of course — but there were other things.

"So it's true, then," Ferdy thrust in sharply. "Danvers Publishing is on the skids. I'd heard that." He lapsed into thought, and then said, more to himself, "Old Mr. Danvers wouldn't touch a book like this."

He turned his strange, light eyes on Paul. Ferdy was no longer vague. He had somehow become harder, even a little taller. It was obvious that his will was not paralyzed by shame, as Alison for the first time suspected that Paul's was.

Had she, with her enthusiasm for the book, brought Paul to this impasse, to this degradation? It was a bitter thought.

"Well, now we know where we stand," Ferdy said cheerfully. "You've got the book I came to buy. But I think that little lady that just went upstairs has a story to tell, too. Go ahead and publish Warwick, Danvers. And I'll put out a rebuttal. A *frank* rebuttal. That will really finish you. And now, I think I'll retire to my room, as they say in the kind of books you used to publish."

Outrageously, whistling, he strolled out of the room with a nod to Alison. The transformation in Ferdy seemed incredible. The world was indeed topsy-turvy.

Paul said fretfully to Lewis, "What do you mean, we're not going to publish it? I tell you —"

"Just tell me, then, and not the entire world. Can't you keep your voice down?"

"How do you know the book won't come out?" Alison found herself saying.

"Because, Miss Monroe, I will not approve any contract for this book. It is a scurrilous attack, without truth, and the lawsuits

102

will be formidable. And if Sessions publishes a really frank rebuttal —" He shuddered slightly at the thought.

Not until much later, when Alison climbed the stairs to her own room, did she wonder how Lewis Hyde — who had read the witty and only slightly malicious first five chapters — could know what lay in the rest of the book. He spoke of an attack without truth, and that must lie in the pages she had not yet read. In — the thought jolted her — the actual events themselves?

The hall on the second floor was lit by sconces set at regular intervals. The deep carpet beneath her feet yielded luxuriously, but somehow it reminded her unpleasantly of plodding through thick sand, pulling her back the more she struggled forward.

It was not the carpet, she decided, her hand on the door knob of her bedroom. It was the undercurrents swirling around her — the heavy emotions, the cross purposes. If thoughts took an actual form, and she believed they did, then thoughts in this house were all daggers floating in the air, like Macbeth's.

She had a mental glimpse, then, of something stirring in the swirling murkiness, lifting and then subsiding. She shuddered in spite of herself. *I don't like it,* she thought, and turned the knob and went into her room.

She touched the switch beside the door and all the lamps turned on at once. There was someone in the room. Something uncurled like a fist in the region of her stomach, but after a moment she could breathe again.

"Sorry," said Eugenia Rice. "Did I frighten you?"

"No," Alison said truthfully. Fright was such a simple word to describe what she had felt. "Feeling better?" she forced herself to add.

"No."

The moments stretched out between them. Alison waited for Eugenia to explain why she had come, but the woman said nothing. She had not removed her makeup, and the rouge spots stood out in irregular shapes against her cheekbones.

Alison turned off the lamp over the desk and the one that gleamed on the tiles in the bathroom, leaving only the small shaded one on the nightstand. The shadows were kinder to Eugenia, and Alison felt she herself could not stand up to much scrutiny.

She pulled a chair up at an angle to the one Eugenia had chosen, and the two sat in near darkness and complete silence for a long time. Alison's eyelids began to droop, and she wished violently that her unbidden guest would depart.

A sudden small sound came from Eugenia, and Alison jerked wide awake. Eugenia was weeping, almost silently, desperately.

"Mrs. Rice!" Alison whispered urgently. "What is it? What can I do?"

It took a long time for Alison to coax the woman to talk. Whatever burden lay on her mind must be lifted, Alison believed, before it broke the woman by sheer weight, and turned her into an easy prey for Ferdy.

"It helps sometimes to talk," Alison encouraged, and at length Eugenia Rice took her advice. Her small voice, rough and yet with a kind of sweetness, spun threadlike in the dim light, telling a tale that Alison thought could only be spectacular fiction.

"You may not believe this," she began, "but once I was happy. It's hard for me to believe it myself. But I was. And I was engaged to a man who was handsome and brave and — dashing, I suppose one would say. All those things. But he had no money."

She fell silent, and at last Alison urged, "Did it matter? About the money, I mean?"

"We thought it did. My mother thought so, and she forbade me to see him. And one night, when it all seemed hopeless —" This

105

time she hesitated only a moment before she continued. "I'm not going to tell you that, even now. You'll find out soon enough. But it was a dreadful temptation and it turned out even worse than I had imagined."

"Worse?" Alison's prompting came as a whisper.

"Nothing less than disaster," Eugenia said simply. "It was a great scandal — all my fault. You don't know how it feels when friends you went to school with snub you in the street. I know that feeling well. My mother collapsed — from shame, she said, and she died."

What kind of scandal? Alison ached to ask. But she only said, "What happened to the man? You married him?"

The woman shook her frizzy curls. "That's what made it all so *useless*. He went away, and I never heard from him again. I think he went abroad. And I moved to New York where I didn't know a soul. But I met Mr. Rice and I married him. I got the money that was so important to me, and — made amends for the trouble I had caused, as much as I could. But by then it really didn't matter anymore."

A familiar story that had to be fiction. And yet the conviction reached Alison that this one was real. There could be no question about the misery that Eugenia was enduring.

"And now, after all these years, the whole thing is going to come out again."

"Jonathan's manuscript?"

"He has no mercy!" Eugenia was frankly sobbing now, and her words were indistinct, muffled by the handkerchief she held at her lips.

Alison could only agree. "How do you know he's going to — to tell the story?" she asked hopefully.

"Because he wrote to me and told me so," Eugenia said dully. Then, with an apparent change of subject, she said, "Did you see that man who arrived just after dinner?"

"No," Alison said. She didn't think it worth-while to relate what she had overheard from the study. "Do you know him?"

Eugenia sat bolt upright in her chair. Her eyes were dark and enormous in her white face. "No!" she cried. "No, I don't!"

Alison put out a hand to calm the woman. Perhaps she shouldn't have encouraged her to unburden herself, not if it led to this near hysteria.

Eventually Eugenia regained a semblance of control over herself, even though Alison judged her restraint was shaky at best.

She rose with a murmured thanks and reached the door before she turned. "If the story all comes out again," she added, simply and very firmly, "I will kill myself."

CHAPTER NINE

After Eugenia had left at last, calmer on the surface, at least, Alison went about her usual routine for bed. Lucky, she thought later, that the procedure was automatic by this time, since she had no recollection of creaming off her makeup, of hanging her dress in the spacious closet, of brushing her hair.

She tugged her flannel robe on, finally, and turned off the light. Snow still hissed at the window, and she was drawn to look at the outside world. It was strange, she reflected, how this last look at the night brought a moment of calm. In the city she had never even been tempted to look at the neon-lit sky just before climbing into bed.

There was little to be seen except the faint gleam of the falling snow, lifted in sheets by the gusty gale, and the vague outline of the trees beyond the lawn. The shape of the landscape was alien and mysterious, as though she had strayed into a fantasy world where every step was fraught with doubt, or even danger.

A stormy night was best for sleeping, she thought, shrugging off her uneasiness. She pulled the curtains open and got into bed.

But Eugenia's misery seemed to linger in the room. Alison revolved in her mind the story the woman had told — or rather, not told. A tale of trouble, perhaps even of crime. But whatever it was, it was a tale of long ago, and there was no need to bring it up now.

Or was there? What could Jonathan gain? Just before she dropped off into a fitful sleep, she recalled that Eugenia had said that Jonathan had sent for her. Therefore, he had a purpose — but what?

Suddenly she was asleep, and yet awake, so it seemed. She stumbled through drifts of snow that were somehow warm, too warm, carrying Eugenia, who was wrapped in purple satin with a turban of green that kept unraveling, snagging sharply on snowy branches.

When she at last awoke, with a start, she did not know where she was. The eiderdown comforter had been kicked off onto the floor — no wonder the snow had felt warm — and the morning sun lay in patches across the grass-green carpet.

The storm was over — at least, the one outside was.

The breakfast table bore signs indicating that she was the last to arrive. But the coffee was still hot, and even as she poured from the silver urn, Emmalu scurried in to clear off the table.

"Scrambled eggs this morning? Oatmeal?" she offered.

Suddenly, Alison was ravenous. At home, her breakfast usually was a glass of orange juice, and later at the office, a sweet roll. Today she said, "I'll have some of everything!"

She tested her waistband secretly. If she were going to eat like a lumberjack, she would have to exercise like one, she decided, resolving to brave the weather. But not until *after* oatmeal and eggs and toast and marmalade.

It turned out that she was not the last to arrive. She was halfway through breakfast when Paul appeared in the doorway. He was freshly shaven, immaculately pressed, and looked almost enameled in his freshness, yet his eyes were tired and worried.

"Didn't you sleep either?" she asked conversationally.

His grunt served as an answer. She must

111

remember that. He was grumpy before breakfast. She filed the information away in her mind, to be brought out when the need arose. But another part of her mind chortled maliciously. What need? Paul is not for you, the imp said. She forced the imp into silence.

At last Paul came to life. He smiled at her, that warming grin that could make her heart turn over, and said, "How soon can we get out of here?"

"I don't know," she said. "It's stopped snowing, but it may have drifted." She remembered that long deep hollow on the road to Crockett. Perhaps there was another road back to town. "You have what you came for?" she asked carefully. "Jonathan signed?"

"No," Paul said shortly. "Lewis is causing difficulties. I don't know what's got into him. Those first five chapters are good, and there's nothing there we could get into trouble over."

"Perhaps it's what's in the rest of the book that you should be cautious about."

Paul eyed her narrowly. "You sound as though this was entirely my problem," he accused. "Are you trying to get out of it? After all, you did talk us all into going ahead with the book."

She stared at him. What had she said? Mentally reviewing her statement, she pounced on the one word that had triggered Paul's outburst. She had said, *you,* not *we.*

"Really, Paul, you're so touchy. I didn't mean anything. You know that what affects you affects me." Then, seeing no answering smile, she insisted, "You do know that, don't you?"

He sought refuge in bluster. "All I know is that the company is going bankrupt and Jonathan Warwick's book can save us. And he won't sign. And Lewis —" He shook his head. It was obvious that he did not know what to think about Lewis.

To her horror, she heard herself asking waspishly, "Why is Sandra here? I didn't think she'd be caught dead in the country."

He got up abruptly and poured coffee for himself and for her. Tell me she doesn't matter, Alison pleaded silently, tell me — again — that you love me. He had said it once — could it be only three days ago? Just after the board had agreed to publish Jonathan.

An obscure little doubt scuttled into her mind. Had Paul only made use of her? The doubt fled almost before she could identify it. Not Paul — not bright, shining, handsome Paul. It would be all right in the end, she told herself. He loved her — he had said so.

Vaguely unsettled nonetheless, she finished her breakfast, and, warmly dressed, made her way out into the snow. The sun was still shining, even though it seemed covered with gray gauze. The fresh air held a sting that made her gasp. But she was soon used to it, and presently she realized that the cobwebs in her mind had been swept away.

The snow lay in drifts. Around the corners of the house, where the wind had held full sway, patches of grass were even visible. But the contours of the land looked different somehow. She realized at last that the hedge at the bottom of the slope was waist-high in snow, making it look oddly shortened.

From far away came the roar of machinery, a snowplow, she guessed. She stopped, listening to it grow louder, and finally she spotted it coming up the driveway.

Such service, she thought. Jonathan even had the highway department working for him. But then she realized that it was the enormous tractor that Dan had been tinkering with, a snow blade attached in front. He was clearing the driveway.

The great mechanical beast paused in front of her. Dan made sweeping gestures with his arm, and suddenly she understood. She ran to him and he pulled her up to stand beside him. He pointed out the hand-holds for her to hang on to — words were useless over the deafening roar — and, satisfied that she was secure, he sent the tractor lurching on its way.

They cleared the driveway, even to the wide space in front of the four-car garage. Then they moved on to a lane leading down to the farm buildings clustered at the bottom of the hill. The wind burned her cheeks and nearly took away her breath.

At last Dan led the tractor into its shed and turned off the motor. The silence was oddly deafening. She had felt the constant jolting right up through the top of her head, but she felt oddly let down now that it had stopped.

"Welded to that bar?" Dan said pleasantly.

She laughed a little, then let loose her handhold and flexed her fingers. "Almost," she said. Then, for lack of anything else to say, she inquired idly about the state of the highway. "Can we get away today?"

A shadow crossed Dan's face. "So anxious to leave?" he asked at last.

The question made her think. She could not honestly say that she was anxious to leave. But what else was there to do?

He didn't wait for her answer. "The road to town isn't clear," he advised her shortly, "and the snow's not over yet either."

"Really?" She looked through the open door to the sky. The sun had vanished, leaving heavy-looking clouds hanging over them.

He came to stand beside her. "Really." She thought suddenly how quiet it was, with no turbulent emotions to unsettle her, no distraught women threatening suicide, no —

"Want to help me with the chores?" Dan asked eagerly, as if offering her a treat.

She dreaded going back to the house. "I'm not good at anything," she confessed, "but I'll try."

It was a strenuous hour, feeding the cattle, fetching straw for their bedding, cleaning out the watering troughs, and chopping away ice. Finally they shoveled snow from the barn doors, so the stock could get in.

And what would they say if they could speak, one night in the year? Judging from their impassive faces, she doubted whether even "thank you" would occur to the black and white beasts.

As for chickens — she never knew there was so much to do for chickens, and she strongly doubted they were worth the effort.

Jerry appeared, to work side by side with her. "Going to snow some more," he said with satisfaction. "That means no pageant."

At last her arms ached and her legs quivered with uncontrollable weakness. Exercise, she thought somberly, I needed. But this?

"Don't you have any help?" she demanded of Dan.

His dark eyes studied her. "We gave the men a couple of days off for Christmas," he explained briefly.

"So I was right," she said bitterly. "Jerry and I are doing the work of half a dozen slaves."

He didn't answer, and when she glanced up at him he was laughing in that soundless way that infuriated her. Impulsively she marched out of the barn. The hard-packed snow, marked with tractor treads, was unexpectedly slippery.

"Alison!" Dan called after her.

When he came up to her, his amusement had vanished. "Alison, be careful."

"How observant!" she marveled. "You saw me nearly fall. Now you warn me that it's slippery. I'm grateful."

"I don't mean the snow. I mean — up there." He jerked his head in the direction of the great house. "Watch your step."

She nearly told him Eugenia's story then.

She wanted to share the burden of it, and she realized to her surprise, that she trusted his judgment.

But it was not her secret to tell, so she kept silent. She didn't even tell him about her vague feeling of growing uneasiness, of an unnamed, shapeless, looming threat.

At length she nodded. "I'll be careful," she assured him.

"Coming back to the house?" he invited.

She looked back at Jerry, standing hopefully in the stable door. "No," she smiled. "Jerry wants to show me some kittens."

With a nod, he left her and proceeded up the plowed lane, leaning into the slope and the rising wind. He paused, halfway to the house, and looked back. He sketched a wave with one gloved hand, when he saw her watching him, and she waved back.

She joined Jerry in the stable. The kittens were of an age to stagger daringly away from their mother, their tiny tails endearingly erect. They were a mixed lot — one black, two yellow, and two with white faces and faint tiger striping, playful and enchanting.

She was charmed, and Jerry tired of the kittens long before she did. She nodded absently when he muttered an excuse and left.

Finally, she became aware of aching knees

and numb fingers. She stumbled to her chilled feet, thinking dark thoughts of pneumonia at the very least. But the quiet of the stable had brought a kind of serenity, and she felt restored to her usual practical self. No more fantasies, she laughed to herself. A capable and competent business-woman, that's what she was. Jonathan's manuscript had been a mistake, that's all. She had learned a lot from this episode, and she would not make the same error again, at least not right away.

Even after she arrived at the house, she was reluctant to return to its stifling heat, at least in her present mood. She wandered slowly around to the front. The pristine snow stretched as far as the edge of the hill, where it met battalions of snow-covered trees, shaking their arms fitfully to rid themselves of their heavy white burden. Far away a sharp crack told of one branch that had given way under the heavy wet snow.

She stood at the edge of the house, listening. There was no other sound. From the chimneys of the house rose gray smoke, dark against the lighter gray of the scudding clouds. The smoke was wrenched from the chimney by the wind, then shredded as it passed over the trees and out of sight.

The scene was lovely beyond words, and

her heart ached with the beauty of it. But suddenly weariness overtook her and she was so cold that she shivered and could not stop.

She ran into the house and took off her jacket. Pulling down the zipper with numb fingers, talking off her fur-lined gloves, stooping to remove the snow-caked boots — all took an unusually long time.

The hall was dark, and her clothes were darker. She must have been unnoticed, she thought later. A small sound caught her attention and she looked up.

The study door was just around the corner from the small alcove where she crouched, one boot off. Jonathan Warwick came out of that door and looked both ways. She was just out of his sight. It occurred to her to make a sound to warn him, but there was something so furtive about his actions that she was compelled to silence.

He passed almost soundlessly down the hall and went into the library. He closed the door behind him so quietly that she guessed he must have turned the knob as he closed it, to avoid the click of the catch.

He had carried something into the library, something that he obviously did not want anyone to see. And it looked to Alison very much like two or three hundred sheets of paper. The rest of the manuscript? The same one he had told Colonel Sawyer was under lock and key in the desk drawer?

Apparently Jonathan thought the strong lock wasn't sufficient to protect the manuscript, and he was removing it to a place of greater safety.

Well, that was his business, of course. But it did nothing to dispel the feeling of impending trouble that enveloped her as soon as she had entered the house.

She had the other boot off now and set them together on a rubber mat just inside the door. It only took a second.

Somewhere, quite close, she heard another sound — the gentle closing of a door, the subdued click of a latch.

Someone else had watched Jonathan move the fateful manuscript. Someone who did not want his presence to become known.

CHAPTER TEN

Alison was not used to such concentrated doses of fresh cold air. Added to that was the fact that she had slept badly the night before, and a wave of compelling drowsiness swept over her after lunch. With only a murmured apology, she went upstairs to take a nap.

Only for a few minutes, she promised herself, slipping off her slacks and sweater and shoes, climbing onto the bed. Just fifteen minutes, she thought, pulling the comforter over her, and she remembered nothing more.

A light tap at the door roused her, and Emmalu was calling, "Are you all right, Miss Monroe?"

It was dark. She turned on the light and called to Emmalu to come in. The maid's eyes were round and frightened. "I called several times," she said. "With everything else going on, I — well, I just didn't like it that you didn't answer," she finished in a rush.

"I'm sorry. I slept like a log."

"All that air," the maid nodded wisely.

"And all that work," Alison added tartly, stretching her arms and feeling the soreness in her muscles. "He's a slave driver."

The maid's remark belatedly caught her attention. "What do you mean, everything that's going on?" She thought of Eugenia's fear, and Jonathan's manuscript, and all the quarrels — anything could have happened.

"I don't gossip, Miss Monroe, but it's not really gossip. It's fact, and I'm sure I don't know how it's all going to end."

Alison waited patiently, choosing her dress for dinner — no choice, really. She had not expected to be here this long.

"I'll run your bath," Emmalu offered, and Alison heard the water pouring into the tub. She wondered whether her sore legs could even get her into the tub — or out again.

"If you knew what I heard —" Emmalu said darkly.

"But I won't until you tell me, will I?"

"Well," she finally said, her voice lowered confidentially, "I saw that Colonel Sawyer and Mrs. Rice — you know, the lady with the stirred-up hair — and they look to me like they were no strangers. A *very close friendship,* I'd say. And she pretended not to know him at first!"

Emmalu looked at her in expectation, waiting for reaction. Alison gave it generously, wondering whether that was all the girl had to tell her.

"But what do you think of that? And the way they acted — well, it's just like that young Mr. Danvers and Miss Hyde. *That close.*"

Emmalu prattled on, not realizing that she had lost her audience. Alison felt oddly cold. For a moment, she seemed to have lost all feeling.

Not until the warm bath water eased her aching muscles, and she began to think again, did she realize that Paul's actions here were all of a piece. He had told her in town that he loved her, held out the promise of a Christmas that might bring wondrous things to pass, but here in Jonathan Warwick's house, he was not the same.

She might make allowances for his worries about the firm, she conceded, beginning to dress for dinner. A little late, one part of her mind taunted. He hadn't worried much when he took over after his father's death. Instead, he'd left too much to the staff. The fact that Danvers Publishing was almost on the rocks was nobody's fault but Paul's.

But worry alone didn't explain his coolness to her.

A sudden rattle of the window startled her, and she went to look out into the night. Pulling the draperies behind her to shut out the light from the room, she peered into a scene that held her fascinated — the great trees beyond the lawn, snowcovered, their tops whipping in the wind.

Wind? More like a gale, sending snow in sheets past her window, and piling up deeply on the sill. The storm had begun again.

All that work with the tractor and the snow plow — all to be done over again before the guests could go their ways — their separate ways.

"If you want something, fight for it," she said aloud. "All right, if we really have something, Paul and I, it's a shame to give it up without a struggle."

She made a few adjustments to her appearance before she went downstairs to dinner, and walked down the stairs with a show of more confidence than she felt.

She found she was ravenous. Dinner was excellent; Mrs. Gibson had outdone herself. Clear soup was followed by salad with a tangy dressing, then roast beef, broccoli with a superb hollandaise sauce, and little cheesy potatoes.

It was lucky that her appetite was good, she thought, for Jonathan was doing his best to ruin the meal for all of them.

He was so gracious about it that only halfway through the meal did Alison begin to hear the needlelike thrusts that lay hidden beneath his words.

"Colonel," Jonathan said, "you must tell us all about your adventures. Were you in the Foreign Legion?"

"No," said the colonel curtly.

"I wonder what could have made me think that?" Jonathan said innocently. "Probably because the Legion is full of men who have something to hide. Remember *Beau Geste?*"

The colonel reddened, and Dan fixed his uncle with a long, grim stare.

"Now Dan," Jonathan said playfully, "just because you're too young to remember that movie — some of us older ones have our little memories. Don't we, Eugenia?" His last words startled the woman. She jumped, rattling her long strings of beads. "Stirred-up hair," Alison remembered Emmalu's description. It did look as if she brushed it with an egg-beater. And that ginger color had to be her own.

"I — I suppose so." She added sugar to her coffee. Alison was positive the brew had already been sugared twice.

"I think the trouble there too was a question of stolen jewels, and Ronald Colman —"

"Stop it!" Eugenia cried. She was standing suddenly, and her coffee spilled over the tablecloth. She paid it no heed, as her eyes fixed on Jonathan. "You're a terrible man," she said quietly, her voice throbbing with the effort to control it, "and why someone doesn't kill you, I don't know."

She threw her napkin down and darted from the room. The rest of the company were arrested in various degrees of shock. At length Colonel Sawyer rose. He had been flushed with anger, but now he was ashen.

Alison and Dan were apparently struck by the same idea. She rose quickly, saying to the colonel, "Never mind, I'll go after her." She heard Dan's voice, calm and steady behind her, and then the babble of voices breaking out all at once.

Eugenia was just vanishing along the second floor corridor. Alison ran up the stairs after her. She thought, I'm not doing very well in my fight for Paul, but it will have to wait.

Eugenia had locked herself in her room.

She would not answer Alison's knock or her calls. At length Alison gave up and slowly went back downstairs.

Jonathan had done this on purpose. What kind of man was he? Alison felt suddenly besmirched, as if a passing car had splashed muddy water on her dress. She wanted nothing more to do with this manuscript. It should be decently buried.

But if Danvers didn't publish it, then Ferdy's firm would take it. And Danvers needed the success.

She sighed deeply when she got to the bottom of the stairs. She had unwittingly set in motion a chain of events that she could no longer control. All she could do — she stopped on the bottom step to consider — all she could do was to ride out the events and try to help where she could.

Someone appeared in the door of the living room, and she looked up to see Dan's worried face. "Is she all right?"

"I don't know. She's locked herself in. Dan, what are we going to do?" It was a natural thing to turn to him for help.

"We?"

She felt her cheeks flushing. "I suppose you had a right to your remarks. I admit, I thought the book was good. But I didn't expect —"

128

"To let loose a herd of scorpions?" he finished for her.

Intrigued, she asked, "Do they come in herds?"

"Hordes, I should have said. Mrs. Rice, and the colonel — I just hope she hasn't put any ideas into the colonel's head."

Alison remembered the heartfelt cry: "Why someone doesn't kill you, I'll never know."

"Is Jonathan upset?"

The sound Dan made could only be called a snort. "Judge for yourself."

He took her arm and led her into the living room. Sandra had cajoled Paul into another endless session of gin rummy. So much for fighting for what you want, Alison thought. Lewis Hyde was coolly remote behind a magazine he had picked up. Ferdy moved aimlessly around the room, eying each in turn, obviously working something out in his mind — how much he could pay Jonathan, Alison thought sourly. She hardly noticed when he left them.

Jonathan looked like a mischievous child who knew he had finally gone too far. He looked up when Alison and Dan entered the room, but apparently did not find what he wanted in their faces. He turned back to his chess board.

But what alarmed Alison the most was the colonel. He sat in an armchair, arranged so he could look at Jonathan. He fixed his eyes somberly and unwinkingly on his host.

The rest of the evening passed somehow, but the colonel never left off staring at Jonathan. At last Jonathan had had enough. He got up, pushing the chessboard away so viciously that the carved ivory men fell in disarray.

"You never did have enough patience," the colonel said tonelessly. "Now, I've had too much, you might say."

"What does that mean?" Jonathan demanded. His attitude was new; he seemed to be daring whatever catastrophe might fall on him to come.

"You'll see," the colonel said darkly. "I'm going up to bed."

He walked out of the room without a good-night. And with his going, Alison thought the tension would ease. But it didn't.

Within moments the company had dispersed, going up the stairs to their rooms — all but Alison. Dan held her wrist lightly, and she didn't wish to pull away. She strongly suspected that his grasp would tighten if she did, and she had no wish for more scenes tonight.

When they had all disappeared, he pulled her into the library, that same room where she had first seen him in the light. She couldn't count that bewitched twilight meeting, could she?

He prodded the fire, sending it leaping into renewed life. He watched it for a long time, until she realized that he had something on his mind that he was reluctant to air.

"You're very transparent, you know," she observed casually.

He looked startled, and swiftly glanced at her. "Really? You know what I'm thinking?"

"You want to tell me to leave, to withdraw the contract. In short, to break faith with your uncle."

To her surprise, he lapsed into that silent mirth that seemed to be a habit with him. Finally he shook his head. "Far from it," he said at last. "Let Danvers go ahead and publish. The lawsuits will keep Uncle Jonathan busy for a while."

She brushed that aside. "That's Lewis Hyde's business."

"So it is," he said slowly. "I wonder —"

"Wonder what?" she said after a long pause.

"Never mind," he said. "I'm so transparent, I shouldn't have to explain anyway."

131

"You're laughing at me."

"Naturally."

"I don't know what you would have done for amusement if I hadn't come," she cried. "I've entertained you for two days now. Perhaps —"

He changed the subject abruptly.

"How much does Danvers mean to you? Is anything settled between you?"

"Why —" she began, but he interrupted.

"What business is it of mine?" he finished for her. "None. But you are a disturbing influence, to say the least. On my uncle, naturally. I *will* be glad to see the last of you."

Irritably he paced back and forth in short steps. She roused herself to retort. After all, taking her cue from him, she could be as rude as she liked.

"After my slaving down there at the barns for you?" she said nastily. "It's the old question of gratitude again. I've had occasion to mention that before, I think?"

Suddenly he was in front of her, pulling her to her feet. His hands moved lightly to rest upon her shoulders.

She never knew what would have happened next, because the colonel burst into the room.

One look at his desperate face, and the fears that she had been able to contain for the moment flooded back at full tide. But she could not have guessed what he would say.

"She's gone!" he said hoarsely. "Eugenia! She's disappeared!"

CHAPTER ELEVEN

Alison moved in a nightmare. From the moment that the colonel burst into the room, surprising her and Dan in their snarling at each other, lurking trouble had turned into disaster.

"Where could she go?" she asked the colonel.

Dan demanded, "What was she wearing?"

The colonel shook his gray head. He looked numb with shock. Alison recalled Emmalu's remark before dinner about his relation to Eugenia. Well, there was no time for speculation now. Find Eugenia.

Alison went to the closet in the hall, to see whether Eugenia's black and white checked coat was there. It hung on its hanger and was dry to the touch. That coat had never been out in the blizzard.

Uneasiness crept up the back of her neck. This was Eugenia's only coat. Could she have been distracted enough to wander out into the snow clad only in her dinner dress?

Sounds from the back of the hall marked Dan's progress in rousing the staff to help in the search. "We've got to make sure she's not in the house," he told the assembled search party, which now included Paul and Sandra. Lewis was not in sight.

Suddenly, Alison was convinced that there was no time to lose. Eugenia, distraught to the edge of lunacy, might have wandered out into the storm. Surely her tracks would show. But even as she delayed, Alison realized the wind was scouring the footsteps into oblivion.

She wasted no time, but slipped into the checked coat in her hand. It was too long, but held a convenient scarf in the pocket. She slipped off her strapped sandals and slid her feet into Eugenia's fleece-lined boots.

As she silently let herself out the front door, she hitched up her skirt with one hand and pulled the door closed with the other. Taking a moment to let her eyes adjust to the darkness, she tried to think where Eugenia would go.

She had not left by the front door, she reasoned. They had all been too close to the hall — in the living room and then later in the library — not to notice. So Alison headed for the back of the house.

Paul and Sandra were no doubt hunting together, she thought. *Well, she's not going to get him — I'll fight for what I want.*

But just now Eugenia came first.

Light filtered out through half-drawn curtains at the windows. It looked as though every light in the house had been turned on. Here in the snow, strange shadows advanced toward Alison and then retreated, like dancers bolted to the floor in a mad ballet.

Just outside the back door that opened to the kitchen wing, she thought she saw footprints. Bending closer to look carefully at them, she decided they were Eugenia's. Since she herself was wearing the woman's boots, this heel-and-toe imprint had to be that of indoor shoes, and who else would have gone out into the snow in high heels?

The wind moaned around the corner of the building with a mournful, lost sound. Urgency was borne on that gale, and Alison followed the only trace of the missing woman she could find.

She followed the tracks a dozen feet, until they reached the edge of the plowed driveway. The blade of the tractor had scraped the roadway flat, but already the edges were indistinct in the darkness, blurred by drifting snow. Which way would the woman have gone?

She huddled inside the coat and tightened the long flowing scarf around her head. She pulled an edge of wool out to protect her face against the wind-driven snow.

Animals always went away from the wind, she had read somewhere, protecting their heads against the buffetting. Eugenia had looked like a stricken doe, Alison thought fancifully — but it was all she had to go on. She turned to her right, away from the house, away from the slope leading downhill to the farm buildings where Eugenia might have sought shelter.

Alison tried to reason as the woman might have — always supposing that she was not driven by blind panic. Escape must have been first on her mind, escape from Jonathan Warwick's insistent prodding, from whatever it was that had driven her to say, "I'll kill myself if the book is published."

What could be in the unfinished chapters?

Head down, Alison plodded along the cleared driveway, scanning the built-up edges of snowdrift for telltale traces of someone climbing over them.

Her memory searched the hundred pages of the script that she had seen. There was nothing about Eugenia in it. Nor was there a word about Colonel Kevin Sawyer. And yet they had both come in desperation to stop the book.

The rest of the manuscript must contain the vital secrets. Jonathan had put the manuscript behind lock and key, and then, in secret, transferred it to the library — observed by Alison and — she remembered the door closing quietly, somewhere — by one other. But how had these people known about what was in the manuscript? Jonathan had written to tell them!

Jonathan was playing a deep and complicated game of cat-and-mouse, she decided, but she could not discern the purpose behind his outrageous behavior. No wonder Dan had called the enterprise wicked.

She paused to listen behind her, to see whether the hunt was over yet. Voices were shouting to each other, then becoming fainter as she listened. Apparently Eugenia had not been found in the house.

She fought the wind, and her scarf. She fought the boots that were suddenly much too big. She could not see in the dim light of reflected snow, and in the end she put her hands out to feel along the snowbank at the side of the driveway. She would follow this side out to the highway, she planned, and then returned by the opposite side.

It was more and more like a nightmare, and yet she knew she could not wake up, walk around the room for a few moments, and return to her warm bed. This was real — and more urgent than anything yet in her life.

Her knees shook and her legs developed shooting pains. Her hands were numb. When they came from the house after the storm was over, she thought wildly, they would come upon two pathetic mounds in the snow, covered with drifts, and probably —

Two mounds? Herself, and — ? Eagerly whimpering a little, she patted her hands over the unaccountable heap of something next to her.

It was! Eugenia lay where she had fallen.

If Alison had exerted herself before, it was nothing compared to what was needed now. Breathing a simple prayer, over and over, she pulled at the body — not body! *Person* — and brushed the snow away. The foolish woman had only a sweater over the dress she had worn at dinner.

When the mound that was Eugenia lay dark against the snow, and Alison's hands were numb stumps of ice from brushing the snow away, she took off the black-and-white checked coat and struggled to get it around the woman, laying it on the ground, and tugging until Eugenia rolled over onto it. Tucking the coat awkwardly into place around her, Alison set out for help.

She screamed Dan's name, but she could hear it torn away from her on the wind. It was several hours — or only as many minutes — before she saw a flashlight beam darting over the ground, approaching swiftly.

"Eugenia!" she panted. "Back there!"

The great yoke of weary responsibility dropped from her shoulders, leaving her giddy. A strong arm steadied her, a heavy jacket was buttoned around her. Feet pounded on the packed snow; there were lights, shouts.

"Is she alive?" she asked, but she received no answer.

Inside the house, the oppressive heat struck her until her head throbbed. She sat on the bench in the hall, numb, unable to move from sheer weariness. The boots pinched her feet, and she couldn't manipulate her hands enough to take them off.

Paul's face swam into focus in front of her, and his fingers fumbled at the buttons on somebody's jacket — Dan's — that enveloped her.

"Come on, now, darling, you're a heroine,

do you know that?"

She found her voice. "Some heroine," she said scratchily. "Where are all the parades?"

"Up and down the stairs," Paul assured her, "ministering to Mrs. Rice. You found her just in time. Another quarter of an hour, and she probably wouldn't have made it."

The jacket was off now and she bent to remove Eugenia's boots. Paul helped her. "Your feet are swollen," he informed her — unnecessarily, since they were pulsating painfully.

He led her into the living room, and she padded alongside him in her stocking feet, leaving little wet marks on the hall floor.

He pushed her into a soft, deep sofa and brought her a small glass of brandy. "Drink it," he urged. "You'll have pneumonia in the morning if you don't."

One swallow was all it took to bring her to life. It coursed through her veins, waking all her senses. She set the nearly full glass down on the table beside her.

Now was her chance to fight for Paul. She had to frame her next words carefully.

"Paul —"

But he was not listening to her. He sat down next to her, his arm across the back of the sofa, behind her. But he did not touch her. "Now then, how did you know where she went?"

"Paul," she began again doggedly, but to her surprise, sheer curiosity dictated her next words. "What's in the manuscript that frightens everyone so much?"

His eyes took on the blank look that always told her that she had gone far enough. But she was anxious to the point of rashness.

"Nothing in the first five chapters would cause all this."

He eyed her narrowly. She could feel his irritation, but she plunged ahead.

"Paul, I think we ought to withdraw on this."

"Withdraw? You've lost your mind. You've seen the bank statements. As it is, this book will have to be rushed through in order to put it on the fall list."

She looked at him as if she had never seen him before. She tried to think what her impression would be if she had met him for the first time. It was difficult, since she knew every expression that flitted across his face — a handsome face, with just a touch of softening of the jawline to reflect a lifetime of good living. The fast sports car she had driven here, and all the other bills the firm had paid — she wondered if he realized how much the shaky condition of the firm was due to his own management.

"It's my fault," he acknowledged, as though his apology would bring an automatic pardon. "But I've got to have that manuscript."

"Ferdy's not trying for it anymore," she told him. She was speaking from pure instinct, and yet she was sure it was true. "He'll get Eugenia's story, and I think he sees more money in that. Paul, I know I urged you to buy Jonathan's manuscript —"

Belatedly he looked at her, adding, "It's all due to you, I know that. Alison, we're a good team. I need someone like you to keep me steady."

"Base flattery," she told him smilingly. But it warmed her more than the brandy had done. So much for Sandra.

He lapsed into his own thoughts and she remained silent beside him. Her imagination told her that this was what the future held for her, a lifetime of sitting beside him, keeping him steady but also sharing. That was the key word: *sharing* his life. It is enough, she told herself. This is what I want.

The fire had died down into popping embers before he roused himself. "Come on," he said, "you've got to get to bed. You're nearly asleep on your feet."

He pulled her up to stand beside him, and kissed her very gently. With an arm around her shoulders, he propelled her to the door of the hall.

Dan was just coming down the stairs, his dark face grim and wary. Emmalu crept behind him like a shadow, holding a basin and a mass of towels.

"She's — she's all right, Dan?" Alison said, stepping forward to look up into his face.

"She'll live," he said briefly. A smile softened his face and was gone again, like a wintry sun flitting over the snow. Strange how she thought in terms of cold and blizzards. "Thanks to you, she will make it," he added.

She started up the stairs, past Dan. She could think of nothing except her bed, hours away up the stairs — at least at her present rate of climbing. But she held it like a grail before her eyes and plodded on. Bed, quiet, soft, sleep . . .

But the night was not over. She was no more than halfway up when Jonathan burst into the hall below her. She thought he came from the back of the house, probably from his study.

"My manuscript!" he cried out. "It's been stolen!"

CHAPTER TWELVE

Dan's hard voice cut through the buzzing in her ears. "Get to bed, Alison," he ordered. "We'll sort this all out in the morning. You too, Mr. Danvers."

"I must say, I don't like your tone," Paul began.

She didn't hear the rest of it, if there was more. She put one foot in front of the other until she found herself looking down at her bed. Mrs. Gibson appeared from nowhere and helped her off with her clothes. The bed was cozy with hot water bottles and the housekeeper's voice came from very far away. "I wonder what Dan's going to do about this. It's the last straw, if you ask me."

Whatever it was . . .

Alison woke, slept, and at last woke again. Day-light, the color of oatmeal, pervaded the room, but it was warm oatmeal, she thought drowsily. Then, in a sort of limbo between waking and sleeping, it all came back to her: Eugenia, the search in the driving snow, and — could it be true that Jonathan's manuscript had been stolen?

It was true, she discovered when she went downstairs to breakfast. Her woolen dress had been sponged and pressed. She must remember to thank Emmalu.

Lewis Hyde was still at breakfast when she entered the dining room. She joined him, noting his horrified look at the amount of food piled on her plate.

Laughing, she said, "I don't know what it is about the country. I've been eating like an army ever since I got here."

"A healthy appetite," he said politely, "argues a clear conscience."

"How is Mrs. Rice this morning?" she asked after the razor-edge of hunger had been dulled. "Could they get a doctor for her?"

"Not in this storm," he said dryly. "I don't know how long we'll be marooned here. I don't even know what possessed me to come."

Now that she thought about it, Alison wondered about that too. There had been no need to oversee the contract, especially if he were simply going to prevent it from being signed. Unless Paul needed his firm hand?

"They have let no one in to see Mrs. Rice," he added, faintly disapproving. "But I understand she is recovering."

"Poor thing," Alison said. She kept to herself the memory of Mrs. Rice and her desperate threat to kill herself. But there was no need to worry, was there? Lewis said the book would not be published, and therefore Ferdy's book based on Eugenia's story would have no purpose. But Paul was going ahead with publication, he said.

She sighed heavily. It was out of her hands. She could do no more. She had talked to Paul, but to no avail.

Her thoughts spoke themselves aloud. "And if the manuscript was stolen —"

Lewis looked at her. He was calm, aloof, as though nothing in the world could shake his self-possession, yet she thought something flickered deep in his light eyes. "*If* that is true, Miss Monroe. After all, we don't know that the manuscript was stolen."

"But Mr. Warwick said —"

"We have only his word for it. Did you have a chance to read the rest of the manuscript yourself?"

"No, but I saw it."

"You did?" A faint smile touched his lips. But the hand that held his coffee cup shook once.

She thought back and finally replied, "No, I can't say that I really saw it. I saw a pile of papers, typewritten, and he *said* it was the manuscript."

Another memory presented itself, of Colonel Sawyer, angry and white, and of Jonathan Warwick, saying, "This lock is strong. If it's broken, I'll know who did it."

But when could he have done it? The timing was hazy in her mind. But she would have to discuss this with Paul.

The faint scent of hyacinth heralded the approach of Sandra. Alison thought with humor that she herself must have slept later than she thought. Sandra's appearance was usually made near noon.

Her arrival put a stop to any further discussion of the manuscript. Lewis lapsed into aloof silence, not unfriendly, but as if his inner self had retreated. After a murmured greeting, Sandra paid him no heed.

Alison had leisure to admire the yellow cashmere pullover that Sandra had chosen to wear this morning, apparently to challenge the gray skies. Outside the snow was still falling steadily now, like a curtain. The wind had died at least for the moment.

How nice it would be, she reflected, to have money — the kind that Sandra had. Those clothes she was wearing would take one of Alison's weekly paychecks, before deductions. That kind of money was part of another world from her own — dashing to the office, putting in a complete day at someone else's beck and call. Surely Sandra must be very content with her life.

"This coffee's too strong," Sandra said. "I can't tell you how glad I will be to get back to civilization."

"Don't you like it here?" Alison asked in surprise. She looked out through the curtain of snow. Veiled in white, the land fell away into coppices of bare trees and rolling fields, until it reached an irregular, forested horizon. She would be sorry to leave, she realized — sorry to return to that constant pressure of her life in the city.

She shook off the idle thought. Of course, she was just as anxious as Sandra to go home.

Lewis departed, pausing in the doorway to give them advice. "Eat well," he said, "today may be trying."

Sandra smiled when he had left. "Well, Mrs. Rice isn't going to pass out on us. I saw that maid in the hall upstairs and asked her."

"What do you suppose made her go out in the storm?" Alison mused. "She was upset, of course — but suicidal?"

149

She wished she had taken Eugenia more seriously. Unfortunately, the woman's jangly necklaces, heavy makeup, and startling hair made her look like a caricature rather than a person. But inside that bizarre exterior, there obviously lay the unhappy person whom Alison had glimpsed more than once.

Sandra broke the brief silence. "When are you going back?"

Alison could be friends with Sandra, she realized with a start. There was an occasional flash of humor in her, and a worldly-wise look in her eyes, like Lewis's.

"As soon as the snow lets up and we can get plowed out." Alison took a deep breath. Now was as good a time as any. "Paul plans to spend Christmas in town with me."

"Good luck," Sandra said flippantly. "But don't count on it." There was no malice in her smile, Alison noted with surprise. It was good-humored, but it was also supremely confident.

Alison faltered. "What do you know that I don't?" she demanded.

"Nothing, really. Except I know Paul, and you don't."

Stung, Alison leaped into battle. "Of course I know him! I work with him every day, and —"

"And into the night sometimes," Sandra finished for her. "I know. But do you know what Paul is really like? What he wants above all else?"

"Of course I do." But Alison's voice lacked conviction. Unerringly, Sandra had put her finger on a sore spot that had never hurt before.

"You know what you *want* him to be like."

"That's ridiculous!" Alison scraped her chair back and stood up. Indignation propelled her words. "I warn you, Sandra. He loves me. And that's all that matters."

"Love!" Her laugh was honest. "Remember what I said. I know what he wants. But I'll wish you luck, anyway."

Not until she had escaped from the house did Alison's anger lessen. She had determined to fight for Paul, hadn't she? And Sandra had accepted the unspoken challenge.

The snow piled up on the steps until they looked level with the porch. She slipped and nearly fell, but she was on her feet again and starting down the driveway.

Yesterday's snowplowing had been foiled, for the snow had covered the road again. Alison floundered in drifts up to her knees. It would be days before she could get back to town. Somehow that thought didn't strike dismay in her heart. She stopped to consider why that should be. She stuck her tongue out to feel the snowflakes falling on it, and heard someone laughing.

Dan waded through the snow like a man through heavy surf. "You look like a kid!" he called.

Kid! Suddenly something was released and she felt like a child. "I'll show you!" she called back, and picked up a handful of snow, molded it quickly, and hurled it at him.

His immediate answer was a scoop of snow in her face, and the snowfight grew in fierceness and hilarity. At last, she ran toward a particularly large deposit of fresh white snow and skidded. Her arms, flailing like windmills, were useless, and she fell backwards into the deep drift, hands and feet in the air.

She lay there for a moment, feeling oddly relaxed. Dan reached her then and pulled her out of the snowbank.

"Truce?" he suggested.

"Truce," she agreed, but could not refrain from adding, "If I hadn't fallen —"

"I know, I know. Not even the cavalry could have saved me."

She giggled. "That was fun."

Surprisingly, it was true. She had lost her

anger in the violent exercise. She would go no farther than that. It was nonsense to think that the gentle contours of the land, the abiding strength of the trees, the spirited fun had anything to do with it.

But if anger had fled, anxiety came to fill the vacuum. No one seemed worried about Eugenia any longer, but the manuscript was still gone — so Lewis had said.

"What is it?" Dan asked softly.

"I just don't understand. Aren't you trying to get the manuscript back? Aren't you trying to find out who broke into your uncle's desk? It would seem to me," she said, warming to her theme, "that you take these things too lightly. You've got a thief in your house — your uncle's house, that is — and you don't care!"

"I'm just the hired hand, a parasite, so to speak. Isn't that what you said?"

Assessing his remark as a diversionary tactic, she waved it aside. "I know," she said with dawning conviction, "it was you. *You* stole the manuscript and jimmied the desk to make it look right."

The amusement in his eyes hardened a little. "I thought you were reasonably intelligent," he said at last. "But you really have no more sense than the Rice woman."

Fury swept over her and her fists clenched

153

hard in her pockets. She could have used a long-handled skillet to advantage, she thought.

"Hitting me won't solve anything," he said, irritatingly perceptive. "The trouble lies in your mind. Too bad. Such a pretty face with not very much behind it."

He sketched a mock bow and left her without another word. She was glad to see the last of him, she fumed, watching him until he was out of sight.

Slowly, reluctantly, she trudged back toward the house. The unaccustomed exercise would mean sore muscles to come, but she ignored that. How dare he say she had no brains?

Finally, she simmered down enough to examine the evidence. What had she done, what had she overlooked, that had given Dan such an impression? Perhaps she hadn't taken Eugenia's declaration seriously enough, but that was not stupid, just a mistake in judgment.

Dan had not called her stupid until after this morning. They had been talking about the theft of the manuscript. Therefore, she reasoned it had to be something about the theft itself.

She had reached the door to the kitchen wing by this time, and stamped the snow from her boots. Inside she teetered on one foot and then the other, taking off the wet boots and placing them neatly side by side on the rubber mat. Darn that man! Now she would have no peace until she had figured out what he had been thinking.

She paused in the door of the kitchen wing and waved to Mrs. Gibson and Emmalu. It took only a moment for her to recognize that some emotion stiffened the atmosphere.

"What's gone wrong?" she asked, advancing into the kitchen.

Mrs. Gibson told her briefly. "It's the pageant. Tomorrow night, and the snow's so bad that nobody thought they could get to the church and *nobody*" — here she bent a fierce glare at Emmalu, who looked away — "did anything about costumes. And now there's not time to get them sewed. That's all. Nothing for anybody to get excited about."

She was obviously quoting Emmalu, whose cheeks flamed with unspoken resentment.

"Don't worry, I'll help," Alison said. "That is, if you would want me to?"

The heartfelt relief on Emmalu's face spoke for her, and she slid over on the bench to make room for Alison. It was later

155

by two fittings of the Wise Men's robes, using Emmalu as model for all three Kings, that Alison dropped the pincushion and the shears at the same instant, and stared around her.

"What's the trouble?" Emmalu demanded resentfully. "You shoved a pin in me."

"Sorry," she answered automatically. "But Dan is right. How stupid can I be?"

CHAPTER THIRTEEN

With a muttered exclamation, she turned and ran out of the room, knowing that Mrs. Gibson and Emmalu stared after her. Somehow it seemed urgent to catch sight of Jonathan going about his daily business, safe and unharmed.

She hurried through the hall, looking in turn into the library and the living room. She was vexed at herself for not having seen at once what was so apparent to Dan.

The manuscript meant nothing!

It could be stolen, shredded, burned, tossed to the winds, for it meant nothing.

What did mean something was that Jonathan still held in his brain all the things that the manuscript might have revealed. And as long as Jonathan lived and moved, the danger still existed!

The door to Jonathan's study was closed, and although she rapped, there was no sound from inside the room. Feeling somehow that she must dash to his rescue, she stood with her hand on the knob, ready to turn it, when someone came in the front door. It was Jonathan.

He peered down the long hall at her. She hoped he had not seen her hand on the knob. She left the door quickly and went to meet him.

"Everything all right?" he said.

"Yes," she said, feeling much more cheerful at seeing him safe. "Has the manuscript turned up yet?"

"No," he said briefly. "I wish —"

She never heard what he wished. He tightened his lips into a firm, thin line, and she thought once again that he was a malicious old man — malicious, but also frightened. And witty, except that now, in retrospect, the manuscript seemed neither witty nor wise.

"How's Eugenia?" he asked.

She told him what she knew and then succumbed to her conscience, which directed her to go at once and inquire. She had neglected the woman, knowing that she was cared for, but she did owe her a visit.

She found that Eugenia was not alone. She was propped up against a mountain of pillows, looking very comfortable, and much more cheerful than she had before. Resignation to fate might have produced a certain peace. And the absence of heavy makeup was a considerable improvement.

Beside the bed sat Colonel Kevin Sawyer, and Alison believed he had been holding Eugenia's hand. He too seemed less troubled.

Alison crossed to the bed and took the woman's hand. "I'm so glad you're better," she said.

"Kevin tells me I owe my life to you," Eugenia said. "I'm so grateful. Yesterday I would not have been, but today —" Her eyes sought Colonel Sawyer's. The conversation idled for a few moments, Alison answering with only part of her attention. Eugenia's eyes never left the colonel, she realized, and at least some good had come out of the whole mess.

Impulsively, she asked, "Why did you do it, Mrs. Rice?"

"Run out into the snow like that? I hope, my dear, that you will never be as miserable as I was."

Suddenly, Alison made up her mind. She had had enough of half-truths, of hints, of shapeless terrors stirring in murky depths. "Tell me, please," she begged. "I'm responsible for this, at least partly. I believed we should publish the book."

"Believed?" said the colonel. "You mean you no longer think so?"

Her doubts instantly crystallized. "That's right. I think it should be suppressed. But I've sold Paul Danvers on it, and now I must unsell him."

"I'm sure you have great influence over him," the colonel commented gallantly. Eugenia's face was unreadable.

"But you must tell me," Alison pointed out, "just what kind of harm publication will do. After all, Jonathan knows whatever he has written, and he can spread it in any way he wants to. But there must be something that publication alone would accomplish."

"I don't want to talk about it," Eugenia said. "It's just so hard to go over it and over it."

"My dear, I think we must," the colonel said gently.

She searched his face, and, apparently satisfied in what she found there, she finally nodded. "You're right. But I'd better start."

The story, once it was pieced together from Eugenia's halting words and the colonel's tender interruptions, was simple enough — a young girl tempted beyond her strength, and an unlucky attempt at atonement.

"You see, Kevin and I were going to be married. Oh, that's ages ago now, probably — no doubt of it — before you were even born. It's hard, I suppose, to think of me as young. I know it's difficult even for me to remember what I felt then. But there wasn't any money. We hadn't a dime between us, and my mother thought I should marry someone who could support us both — Mother and me, I mean."

"But Eugenia refused to do that," commented the colonel, with a smile. He had crossed to the window.

"I couldn't imagine not marrying Kevin," she said, "and it was such a strain, trying to stand up to my mother, and sneaking out to see Kevin, and going to lots of dances and house parties just because I knew I'd see him. But every time I saw him," she ended, lifting her hands helplessly, "it was harder to leave him."

The colonel came back to stand beside the bed and touch Eugenia's cheek with a gentle finger. "Don't cry, my dear. That's all past."

Suddenly the tears flowed down the pale cheeks. "It will never be over, Kevin. Never!"

Awkwardly, he patted her shoulder. Alison sensed that her presence was awkward, but she could not bring herself to leave.

"My dear, I have promised you there's nothing more to worry about."

How could he be sure? Alison wondered. Jonathan could still speak, Ferdy was anxious to unearth Eugenia's story, and — she glanced upward at the colonel and surprised a look on his face that unnerved her. The colonel was a ruthless man, she realized, one who did not lightly promise what he could not produce.

Eugenia had taken up her story again. "One house party we went to — never mind whose it was — was after my mother had announced my engagement to someone else, not Kevin. It seemed as though this was the last time Kevin and I would ever see each other." She leaned toward Alison and took both her hands in her own. "I don't know how I can make you see how very desperate I was. If you ever fall in love, maybe you will know."

Alison murmured, "I am in love."

"Enough to steal for him?" Eugenia said wryly.

"Steal!"

Eugenia nodded. She cast a look at the colonel's back. He stood at the window again, fiddling with the cord on the venetian blinds. She sighed heavily. "I went upstairs to powder my nose, and there on the small vanity in my hostess's bedroom lay her emerald bracelet."

Alison's heart sank. If Jonathan had decided to put this in print, libel suits would bristle like a picket fence — to say nothing of the heartache that would follow. This was real grief, not something to read about between hard covers of a book.

"And I took it." Eugenia's voice had gone flat.

"She took it for me," the colonel said.

"For us," Eugenia corrected. "But of course I no sooner had it than I knew it was no good. To get money that way, I mean. So I wanted to give it back, but I never had a chance."

Colonel Sawyer took up the story then. "The house party broke up at once. Everyone knew the bracelet was gone. And everybody watched everybody else. There was no chance to restore the emeralds to their proper place. So Eugenia gave the bracelet to me, trusting me to return it."

"But something went wrong," Alison guessed. She had not realized how tense she was, how gripped by the story. She moved slightly, and a pain shot through her cramped leg.

"Something did indeed go wrong," Colonel Sawyer said. "I gave it to — someone — to return for me. The bracelet was never seen again."

"What do you mean? Didn't he return it?"

"He said —" Colonel Sawyer tossed the cord away from him with a sudden spurt of irritation and came back to stand at the bedside. "He said I never gave it to him. That he had never seen the bracelet."

"Leaving you," Alison said slowly, "to carry the blame."

"Branded as a thief, he was!" Eugenia said indignantly, "when all he had done was try to help me!"

She began to cry again, but she must have spent most of her grief, for only two teardrops ran down her cheek.

"Now, dear," he said, "I told you I'll take care of it. He can't hurt us anymore. We'll go some place far away."

Finishing quickly, the colonel told Alison that he had gone abroad, hiring himself out as a mercenary soldier — sort of a one-man Foreign Legion, he said with an attempt at humor — and earned his rank as colonel in some army in the depths of Africa, as it happened.

"But if Jonathan had the bracelet —" Alison said in slowly dawning horror. Both the others interrupted her: "Not Jonathan!"

164

"But who?"

Not another word could she get from the two, who now plainly wished her to be gone. They had unfinished business of their own to take care of, and she was in the way.

She left the room. The story she had heard was wild and romantic, she admitted, but heart-rending just the same. And she must not let Paul publish the book.

At last she found Paul, sunk in a chair in the living room. Lewis sat before the fireplace. The attorney had pulled a small table in front of his chair and he was obviously carrying on his business. The briefcase half open at the side of his chair, the pile of papers and blue-backed legal documents before him, and an air of abstraction as though he disdained his surroundings and had escaped into his secret world of deeds and torts, made him even more remote than usual.

She crossed the room to sit down next to Paul, and spoke in an undertone, so as not to disturb Lewis. "Paul," she whispered urgently, "this whole trip up here is my fault. But I don't want us to publish the book."

"Not publish?" Paul eyed her sourly. "No woman understands business. I keep telling you, the bank is foreclosing."

"We'll think of something else," she said, brushing banks aside. Cannily, she added, "the lawsuits will cost money — money we don't have."

His suspicions were aroused. "What's changed your mind? That farmer?"

Blankly, she stared. "Farmer?"

"The old man's nephew."

"Nonsense. Not him. He couldn't change my mind —" Too late, she realized this was a false trail. But she stopped short of admitting that the "farmer" had told her she didn't have a mind to change. That was nobody's business.

"I've simply changed my mind," she stated with dignity. "It's too hot a script for us to handle. Danvers has never gone in for this kind of book." She was aware that she was arguing against her own previously held opinions, but she couldn't help that.

"Danvers has never been this broke," Paul said, adding, "You know something, don't you?"

She could not meet his eyes. She would not tell him Eugenia's story. There was something that she still did not know about it, and that was who had taken the bracelet, and denied having it. It was all of twenty-five years ago, but somehow it seemed to her as though it were just now happening, that she could search the coats in the hall closet and bring out the glittering green jewels.

"Besides," he said craftily, "I may not have to publish it."

"Paul! You mean there's another way to save the company?"

He nodded. "Now don't ask questions. Be a good girl and run along."

She thought he was going to kiss her, and that he refrained because of Lewis Hyde's presence. But when she rose to go, she saw that the lawyer was no longer there. She didn't know when he had left.

Suddenly lighter in heart, knowing that there was another way to save Danvers, she walked to the door. She turned and looked back.

"Paul, we may not get to spend Christmas together in town, but we'll be back by New Year's, won't we?"

He hesitated as though he had been lost in his own thoughts. "What? Oh, yes, New Year's for sure."

She lingered, but he said nothing more, so she went into the hall. What was Jonathan's reason for relating the story of the bracelet? She had not read the actual script, but he had written to both Eugenia and Colonel Sawyer to tell them he had included the incident in his memoirs. To what purpose?

Colonel Sawyer had said to Eugenia, "Don't worry, I'll take care of it." How? Persuasion was not a potent weapon in dealing with Jonathan.

But she had one in her own hand. Paul Danvers might not publish the book, so Jonathan could find another way to tell the story, if he were determined.

She went down the hall to his study. She did not have a clear idea of what she was going to tell him. But the picture she saw when she pushed the door open into that lovely pristine room would remain clear in her mind for the rest of her life.

Smoke poured from the fireplace behind Jonathan. Jonathan himself was seated at the table, his back to the fireplace, facing her. His eyes were shut, and a long red stream the breadth of a lead pencil inched down his forehead to join the patch of shiny, wet blood covering the side of his face.

And while she watched, he slowly fell forward almost deliberately, to lay his head on his crossed wrists.

His fingertips were bloody, and the top of his head was an odd color, for his gray hair was mixed with dark, glistening blood, where someone had struck him a vicious blow.

She screamed, and screamed again.

CHAPTER FOURTEEN

It was still snowing. She would not have believed that the sky could hold so much moisture. She looked dully out the living room window, watching the flakes fall relentlessly, listening to the strained fragments of conversation behind her.

Jonathan had been carried to the leather davenport in his library. She had stayed with him until the doctor had arrived from Crockett by way of the county snowplow, and making the last leg, the driveway, on snowshoes.

She could still see Dan's grimly forbidding face, his lips compressed into a thin line as he returned to the library to say briefly, "The doctor's coming."

That was two hours ago. But the picture remained as vividly in her mind's eye now as it was then, of Jonathan's bloody fingertips as she gently brushed them with a wet towel, trying to clean up the worst of the mess. After she had screamed, Dan had been at her side on the instant.

"Where did all the blood come from?" she had said.

"His head," Dan said at once.

She looked more carefully at the unconscious man. A long cut on his cheekbone had bled profusely. His temple was darkly bruised, but his hair was so matted that she shuddered and turned away, her stomach convulsing.

Now, in the living room, waiting to hear the doctor's pronouncement, she felt suspended in time, with the snowfall outside reminding her of a paperweight she had had as a child.

Even Eugenia had roused herself to come down to share the vigil. Colonel Sawyer was unobtrusively at her side — whether for company or protection, was not clear.

Sandra seemed unusually watchful. Her eyes darted between Paul and her father, but she seemed to find no comfort in either.

"I wish I'd never heard of the manuscript," Alison said at last, breaking the waiting silence. "I was wrong. I should have sent it back at once."

It was the nearest she could come to an apology to Paul, at least with the others watching avidly.

Colonel Sawyer rumbled, "What good would that have done? He sent for us, really. At least for Eugenia and me. But I'll admit —" He turned his head toward the door, as if he had heard something.

Lewis, standing just inside the door, looked briefly into the hall. "There is no one out here."

"I wonder if he's dead," Sandra said, startling them all.

"No," Alison said. "I don't think so."

"You found him, didn't you?" said Lewis Hyde. "How odd." He managed to invest his words with an insinuation that she resented.

"Yes," she retorted. "He — he fell over onto the desk just after I went into the room."

"Then you didn't see who hit him, did you?" It was Eugenia, her voice still weak from her ordeal, but the worry in it was strong.

The question was out in the open at last. Each in his own way, they had all skirted the ugly fact of guilt — by ignoring it, by getting angry, or by neat thrusting at someone else.

Now it had been spoken: someone had attacked Jonathan Warwick, had viciously struck him down with a weapon not yet found, and with intent to kill him.

"No," she said firmly. "I saw nobody."

"But it had to be one of us," said the colonel. Eugenia's hand shot out to touch his sleeve. Enjoining silence on him, Alison wondered?

She considered each of them in turn. Paul had been in the living room with her. And so had Lewis — but no, he had been gone when she left the room. But only a few moments before? Had there been time? That was laughable, she thought, looking at the imperturbable attorney. He would not need to act with violence. But Eugenia obviously thought that Colonel Sawyer had gone to Jonathan, pleaded with him perhaps, and then, seeing that Jonathan was adamant, struck him.

Of all the persons in the room, Alison decided, only Colonel Sawyer had lived a life of violence. And he had twenty-five wasted years to exact payment for. Whoever had accepted the emerald bracelet from Kevin Sawyer, and then denied it — that person could not be Jonathan. Both Eugenia and the colonel had cleared him. Besides he surely would not have brought the ugly incident to light again if he were guilty.

No. And now she realized what she should have known at the start. There was an odd

173

whiff of blackmail somewhere in this tangle. *And if Jonathan dies, then it's murder too.* She did not know she was speaking aloud.

A wild cry rent the air. Eugenia had struggled to her feet, throwing off Colonel Sawyer's restraining hand. "I did it," she cried wildly. "I hit him. It's my fault!"

Her words died away in sobs. But even after Colonel Sawyer had gently guided her from the room, shaking his head at Alison, who had started forward to help, the desperate sobbing lingered like a tangible presence.

Paul got to his feet. "I can't stand this anymore," he said to no one in particular, and made for the door. Lewis stood aside, and the two men exchanged long looks before Paul dove into the hall. Lewis murmured an apology and followed him, at a more leisurely pace.

"Well, Alison?" Sandra said at last. "We're the only survivors."

"Eugenia didn't hit that old man," Alison said sharply. "She's protecting the colonel."

"You think the colonel did it?"

Alison raised her eyes slowly to look at Sandra. "What do you care? You're not part of this trouble. It's all my fault."

Sandra rose and crossed to the table to lift a cigarette from the box. "Come on now, don't be a martyr," she said dryly. "Unless you lifted your hand and nearly killed an old man, you are not to blame. And I don't think you've got courage enough for that."

"Courage? Ha! It wouldn't take much. He's the most vicious —"

Her voice died away, and there was silence for a long time. The smoke from Sandra's cigarette rose lazily, and the logs in the fireplace fell with a soft plop as they burned through.

"Alison? Thought any more about what I said?"

Alison stared blankly. "What do you mean?"

"About knowing what Paul is like. About giving up on thinking that he's going to marry you."

"And you know him better than I do, I suppose?"

Sandra shook her head in disbelief. "Alison, Alison — how can you think otherwise? Why did he come down here? Do you know that?"

"To help me get Jonathan's signature on the contract," she said sturdily. "To help *me*."

"There," Sandra said enigmatically. "That's the first thing, right there. That's not the reason he came. Think about it."

This was the second time in less than a day that she had been accused of stupidity. Was she naive? When she looked up to demand that Sandra answer her own question, the girl had gone. She was alone.

She could not stand her own thoughts. A surge of restlessness brought her to her feet and finally led her to the hall. She walked to the front door and looked out. The snow seemed lighter, she decided. But her thoughts were still heavy.

Could Sandra be right? Could it be that she, Alison, did not understand Paul? And what difference did it make anyway? Understanding was not the same as loving.

Sandra had suggested that she could give Paul what he wanted. But what was that? Understanding? Maybe. Devotion? No more than Alison could. Social success? Undoubtedly.

But only Alison could give him Jonathan's book. And that was what Paul wanted and needed to save Danvers Publishing. And — face it, Alison — that is what you will do everything you can to keep him from having.

Weary at last, she went back to the settee in the hall and slumped down on it. She had brought trouble to Jonathan, and more than trouble to herself. But what it was that had happened to her, she did not know yet. What she badly needed was her own apartment around her, the traffic noises muted in the snow, with nobody to talk to her, to bring up questions that she didn't want to think about.

Who said there was peace and quiet in the country?

She was not inclined to move — where would she go? — so she was still sitting there when the doctor and Dan emerged from the library.

"No need to take him in for X-rays," the doctor was saying. "Not under the circumstances."

What circumstances? Was he so near death it didn't matter anymore?

The doctor added, almost cheerfully, "It's the best way out. You know that."

Dan nodded crisply. "I couldn't agree more."

How ghoulish! Waves of disgust alternating with nausea swept over her. She controlled her tongue until the doctor had put on his snowshoes, stepped out to the front porch, and Dan had closed the door behind him.

"I thought I'd seen everything!" she announced in a low, vibrating voice. "Now you can take over your uncle's farm, and —"

she stopped short, seeing by his grim, set expression and his flashing eyes that he was furious. If he had struck down his uncle —

She watched Dan as he made a heroic effort to control his anger. At last he managed to say, in a strangled voice, "You think I would raise my hand to my uncle? You really have that low an opinion of me?"

She could give him no answer. She knew she was wrong, that the man who was so gentle with livestock, and protective of the embarrassed boy she had seen that first night, could not strike the brutal blow that had brought Jonathan as near death as the doctor had hinted. But she could not tell Dan this.

"I wish you had never come here," Dan said, with surprising bitterness. "I don't suppose you meant to unsettle — things." Abruptly his face closed against her. She knew that he meant more than he had said, but now she could find no key to his thoughts.

"You'd better come with me," he said, frost edging his words, "and see what a villain I really am."

He took her into the library, where Jonathan lay, still as death, on the brown leather davenport. His head was heavily bandaged, and his face was nearly as white as the gauze. The cut on his cheek was covered by bandages.

"Stay with him, will you?" Dan said crisply. "I've got some business to take care of."

She sat alone with the injured man for what seemed to be a long, long time. Suddenly she became aware that the rhythm of his breathing had changed. She looked sharply at him, to find that he was awake and looking at her.

"Dan says you found me," he said tentatively. His voice was very weak.

"That is true."

"I was hit," he said firmly.

"How do you feel now?"

There was a slight sound at the door behind her. Apparently it did not disturb Jonathan. He looked at her with a faint frown between his eyes. Under his gauzy turban, his eyes turned suddenly vague and watery.

"Who are you?"

She gaped at him. "Why, I'm Alison Monroe," she told him. "I came from Danvers Publishing with the contract. Don't you remember?"

His voice was suddenly much stronger, filling the room. "No," he said, too loudly. "I can't remember anything. That blow on my head — I've lost my memory, the doctor says."

She regarded him skeptically. "Lost your memory? Then you can't finish the manuscript?" He was so obviously far from being seriously injured that she felt oddly tricked. "That's convenient for you, isn't it?"

He beckoned her closer, and whispered, "Safer, my dear." He underlined his meaning with a vast wink.

Why, you old fraud! she thought indignantly. All my worry, all the misery he had caused Eugenia, whatever dark deeds he might have inspired in Colonel Sawyer —

And the damage he has done to my love for Paul, she realized, no one could ever know.

She regarded him with growing disgust that she didn't try to hide. A petty man, and how he could even be related to Dan —

Jonathan quickly read her expression. He closed his eyes at once and began to breathe heavily, as though in sleep. Unaware of time, she allowed her thoughts to travel where they would — Jonathan's lost memory, Colonel Sawyer's unveiled threats, Paul's hints of rescue for Danvers Publishing from a new source —

There was no sense in any of it. The chair was deep and comfortable, and after awhile she dozed. When she woke, something that had nibbled at the edge of her dream stood out in sharp focus.

Deliberately she placed herself back in the white study, when she had discovered Jonathan. The smoke — yes, that was it. The smoke pouring from the fireplace behind Jonathan! And as they had moved the injured man, she had glanced at the fireplace, and now her memory obligingly dredged up the identity of the object lying in the flames.

The manuscript! The stolen manuscript!

She must tell Dan at once. He would know what it meant, whether Jonathan had discovered the thief. It did not occur to her until much later that she had not once thought of telling Paul of her discovery.

Emmalu was in the hall. "Isn't it great news?" the girl cried.

Alison could not think what the girl meant. Emmalu kindly explained. "The snow is stopping. And the pageant will go on after all, and we'll —"

Her voice died away. Belatedly she remembered old Jonathan Warwick. "How is he?" she asked in a heavy whisper.

"All right, I guess. All bandaged up. Where is Dan, do you know?"

"He's got them all in the living room. He's

trying to find out who hit old Jonathan. I mean, Mr. Warwick. And he sent me to go and sit by the patient," she finished importantly.

The living room was indeed full. All the members of the house party, so to speak, were assembled. Dan stood at the fireplace like a lecturer facing his class. Sandford held the door open for her as she quietly slipped in, then he closed it behind her.

Dan looked up when she came in and nodded impersonally. Where was the gay, boyish person who romped in the snow with her? And, she thought ruefully, where was the girl who had then been lighthearted enough to gambol with him?

"It's all out in the open now," Dan said. "The manuscript has been found — burned, but not completely destroyed."

"Who burned it?" Paul said hoarsely.

"Don't you know?" Dan replied softly.

Eugenia startled them all. "I know who did. I saw her. I went into the study, but Jonathan was not there. She was burning something. You!"

She pointed at Sandra, who, for the first time that Alison could remember, turned pale, her eyes darting around the room to rest on Paul.

"And what I want to know is —" Eugenia

leaned forward accusingly in her chair to face Sandra, "did you read it first?"

Chapter Fifteen

There was a babble of voices after Eugenia's strident accusation, but Dan's firm tone cut across them.

"I think," he said calmly, "that there is no danger in what Miss Hyde read in that manuscript. No danger to anyone."

Alison felt that she had long ago lost any understanding she might have had of what was going on. She glanced at Paul. His face wore an odd mixture of surprise, and something else. If she didn't know him so well, she would think that other element might be guilt.

Sandra had recovered her usual self-assurance. Apparently she could admit to stealing and destroying a valuable manuscript with as much casual confidence as it took to have her hair done.

"Actually," she said, "the manuscript *was* a surprise. But I didn't steal it, of course. Ferdy did."

A black glare was her reward from Ferdy Sessions. "She's right," he said harshly. "The fraud of a lifetime. A hoax! But I thought she could find a use for it." He shrugged.

"A great disappointment," Sandra said. "There was nothing in the manuscript."

"Nothing?" cried Eugenia, and Colonel Sawyer swiveled in his chair to look at Sandra with skepticism. "He didn't tell —"

"He told nothing," Sandra said. "It was a great disappointment to Paul when he found out that the manuscript that was supposed to save the firm turned out to be nothing but blank pages." She glanced triumphantly at Alison.

"Sandra! You're wrong! I saw it myself and the pages were not blank," Lewis Hyde exclaimed, jolted out of his aloof pose.

Sandra looked aghast but Dan's voice cut smoothly across the confrontation between Lewis and his daughter. "And when did you see that manuscript, Mr. Hyde?"

Too late, Lewis saw the pitfall yawning beneath his feet. Alison cast her mind back over the sequence of events that afternoon. If Lewis had stolen the script the day before, he would have read it. But he said only that the pages *were not blank.* So the script must already have been in the fireplace when he first saw it. That left Sandra in the clear. She had set it afire, Eugenia had seen her, and Jonathan had not been there.

Lewis must have then come in after his daughter had left, seen the script in the flames, and snatched a few pages from the fire. The pages Alison had seen, browning in the flames, were not blank, but the typing was already illegible from the heat.

And that was what Lewis had seen — it had to be.

"Mr. Hyde is the one who struck my uncle," Dan pointed out, "and that heavy ring on your finger is what did the damage."

"I wasn't anywhere near the study at any time," Lewis said calmly, as though the idea that he would have to account for his time was absurd.

Dan's voice was pleasant. "I suppose that ring has been washed, but I wonder what a laboratory examination would show. Blood has a way of being hard to wash away."

For a moment Lewis looked disconcerted, but when he spoke again, his voice was as bland as ever. "I have a witness to my whereabouts, at all times. I was here in the living room with Paul until the young lady screamed."

Alison listened indifferently, until her

memory cast up a scene. When she had left Paul, she had been surprised to find they were alone. Lewis had left his papers behind, but he himself was not in the room.

Lewis was watching her. "I left only to wash my hands. And Paul will tell you so."

Paul was less than enthusiastic. But he nodded, saying in a low voice, "That's right. He couldn't have done it."

Alison was indignant. Of course he could have done it. Paul had no notion of how long Lewis was gone. And it would only take a moment to strike down an old man, if you took him unaware while he was trying to retrieve his manuscript from the flames.

Studying Sandra's face, Alison was suddenly convinced that Sandra had lied about the blank pages. But there were bigger stakes than the manuscript now. Lewis himself was proof of that, as he watched Dan with wary eyes.

"Why?" Dan was saying. "Was it you who had so much to lose, was it your name — Lewis Hyde — that was laid out in print for everyone to see, and wonder where the emerald bracelet had gone?"

Colonel Sawyer nodded. "I gave the bracelet to him, and he denied it," he said heavily. "It ruined my life, and took Eugenia away from me. And yet, I can't feel that anything matters anymore, now that I have her back."

Alison's indignation surged into speech. "You mean that Lewis Hyde kept the bracelet? And sold it? And today Paul lied to give him an alibi?" Her voice dropped to a shocked whisper. She looked mournfully at Paul, her love. No, she corrected herself carefully. The image of Paul that she had built up in her mind was what she had loved.

No matter. She would have to deal with that later, alone.

She needed to get out. She could see Sandra's cool, contemptuous eyes assessing her, and she knew that she'd been a fool. Mustering what dignity she could, Alison marched to the door. On the threshold she turned to look back at them all.

"You're a fine bunch," she said, burning the last bridge behind her. "Grand larceny, arson, assault with a deadly weapon — all in a day's work for Danvers Publishing?"

Sandra had won. Some time in the future, it would not matter, but just now it did. It mattered very much.

She heard footsteps behind her in the hall. It was Paul.

"Look, Alison —" he began.

"Look at what?" she countered. "The spectacle of a man without a backbone? How did it happen?"

"I had to give him an alibi," Paul said. "Sandra told me the manuscript wouldn't save Danvers, because there was nothing in it."

"So?" Alison said.

"So Lewis is going to put up the money I need, by becoming a partner."

"Partner is the word for Sandra, too, I suppose?" she said in glacial tones. She could have added, but didn't, that now she saw the reason for Sandra's pursuit of the manuscript, why she had burned it — to discredit the junior editor who had staked her career, and happiness, on Jonathan Warwick.

"I had to do it, don't you see?" Paul was pleading for understanding, for forgiveness for his betrayal.

She couldn't give it easily, but, with sudden clarity, she saw that Sandra did indeed understand Paul and what he needed, and she herself did not. And she at least said the words he wanted to hear.

"It's all right, Paul. Believe me, I do understand."

But she could not stay in the same room with him. Perhaps with time and distance, true forgiveness might come. Just now —

She turned her back on him. There was no place else to go but the library. So she turned the knob and entered, leaving Paul standing alone in the hall with whatever conscience still struggled within him.

Emmalu was glad of the escape that Alison furnished her. Left alone with the patient on the davenport, Alison sat in a nearby chair, feeling the chill of numbness overtake her. She had arrived with such high hopes, with the touch of Paul's lips on hers, with the promise of a Christmas together still lingering in her ears. And what had she got?

Well, she thought, I won't think about that. Not until I'm alone in my own house with the phone off the hook.

Sandra had won. That was all there was to it. True, she had used devious methods, and worse, but they had worked. And they would not have worked unless Paul had been willing. Some men could have resisted the petty temptation of the Hydes, father and daughter.

Some men — she thrust the thought of Dan out of her mind. But he would not stay on the shelf where she had put him. She was humiliated now, remembering her accusations against him. Why, it must have been Dan who had been keeping an eye on everyone's actions all along.

"Trouble?" said a surprisingly strong voice

from the davenport. "I see you're clenching your fists."

She looked with startled eyes upon the supposedly weak patient struggling to sit up. "I'm sure my nephew has straightened the whole problem out now. Hasn't he?"

"Perhaps he has," Alison said, "but I don't know what there is to straighten out. They're all angry with you because of your book. And now it turns out there's no book at all."

"No," Jonathan said. "Pages of harmless, long-winded memories of an old man. I just wanted to make Lewis Hyde squirm a little, like the worm he is."

"That business of the bracelet?" Alison hazarded. "Was he truly the one who had it last?"

"Oh yes, he was. But that wasn't all. There was something he did to me once that I didn't want him to get away with. But the situation got slightly out of my control, with the colonel's threatening letters, for one thing."

"Then," Alison picked her way carefully, "you never even had a book? You just used me to get Lewis Hyde down here?"

Unexplained details were suddenly clear: his knowledge of Lewis's name and position, his anxiety for the Danvers lawyer to come down.

"But it's all so messy. I didn't want to hurt Eugenia or Kevin. I knew them back at the time of the theft, you see, and I thought the owner of the bracelet had asked for trouble, leaving such a valuable thing lying about. I thought if Eugenia and Kevin came, and Lewis too, he would be . . . a little worried. How I wanted to see that! But it all got too sordid."

To say nothing of what Jonathan's caper has done to me, Alison thought mournfully.

"But," she roused herself to point out, "Lewis did hit you?"

"And the thing bled so badly, and all of a sudden I saw how I could get out of it. I smeared the blood into my hair, and Dan and the doctor went along with it. Lewis thinks I've lost my memory, and the manuscript is destroyed, so I'm out of it all."

The smile on the bruised face was innocent as a child's. Once he had said he was sorry, Jonathan obviously believed the incident was erased.

She got up. He didn't need anybody to take care of him, not any more. It was all those around him who needed help, she thought bitterly

"Why did you tell me all this?" she asked.

"Because, the one good thing that has come out of this is you," he said in a burst of honesty. "And I don't want our future clouded by mistrust. We'll be seeing a lot of each other, you know."

She looked down at him, not troubling to disguise her dislike. "That," she said crisply, "will be the day."

In the hall she found that much had happened in her absence. She glanced at her watch. She was shocked to find that two hours had gone by. In that time, Paul, Lewis, and Sandra had packed, and now stood with their bags in the front hall. Sandford was industriously fussing over their departure, as though he couldn't wait to see the end of them. Alison, feeling her face drawn into unfamiliar lines, agreed enthusiastically.

Ferdy left almost without a word, and Colonel Sawyer was not far behind. "The plow has cleared the road," he told her in an aside. "Eugenia is going to stay here over Christmas. I have to visit my niece, but I'm coming back," he announced shyly, his face looking more than ever like a terrier's, one who had found a satisfactory bone.

The bustle of leavetaking was over at last, and Alison felt as if they had been her own unwelcome guests. She relaxed when she saw the last of them.

Dinner was early — "for the sake of the

pageant," Mrs. Gibson had told her. Astoundingly, it was Christmas Eve.

"I hadn't thought about Christmas for two days," she said to Dan. "It doesn't seem possible that it's here. Or that you've invited me to stay."

She had been grateful for that invitation to her and to Eugenia. She hadn't really wanted to go back to her own apartment to spend Christmas alone, not after her hopes of Paul's company. She would have to deal with her heartache and disillusion, but it could wait. The prospect of Christmas here with the Warwicks was not what she would have chosen, but it was enough. With Jonathan confined to his room upstairs to recover from his minor injuries, there was almost a feeling of gaiety downstairs.

Ferdy's theft of the manuscript, his turning it over to Sandra in disgust, and Lewis's assault on Jonathan — such a welter of crime, and nothing could be proven.

Dan said quietly, "It goes against the grain to see them all drive off scot-free." He turned to look at Alison. "But they have to live with themselves, and that's punishment enough."

She couldn't agree, not then. But there was nothing she could do, and, seeing Eugenia watching her anxiously, she put her own thoughts aside and smiled at the woman.

"This is the first Christmas in years that I expect to enjoy," Eugenia confided. "Kevin and I are together again. My dear, you'll never know what an escape you had from that dreadful publisher. His eyes were too close together."

Alison forced a smile. Eugenia deserved a season of happiness, and Alison firmly shoved her own troubles into a closet in her mind and turned the key. "Let's dress for the pageant," she said. "I almost know the whole thing by heart, myself."

Later that day the station wagon was heavily loaded as they drove along the plowed road. Eugenia, Mrs. Gibson, and Emmalu sat in the seat behind Alison and Dan. In the very back Jerry perched among boxes of costumes.

The night slipped by outside, eerie and white, and the tire chains sounded remotely like sleigh bells. Gradually she felt the hurt easing — not going away, but at least stirring, as though it might, someday, be gone.

Conversation was muted, and silence fell more than once. Finally Mrs. Gibson said, "Dan, you'll have to get someone to take Sandford's place."

Alison became alert. Sandford was leaving?

"Got any ideas?" Dan asked.

"Emmalu's young man. You'd get along all right if he was around."

Dan glanced sidelong at Alison.

"But I thought Sandford was devoted to Jonathan?" Eugenia said.

Dan was plainly grinning. "My uncle Jonathan thinks that this country is no longer healthy."

"Maybe his memory will return," Eugenia said tightly, "with the stimulation of new places."

"His memory will never return," Dan assured her. "I can guarantee it."

Mrs. Gibson added a tart comment. "He's even forgotten that he was pretending to own the farm. You put up with a lot from him, Dan. I say he's a lucky man to have a nephew like you, letting him live there and put on all those airs."

Alison sat, stunned. Was there no limit to Jonathan's fraud?

"You'd better take advantage of it," Mrs. Gibson added, "and get married. Then if Jonathan wants to come back, there'll be no room."

Alison felt battered, almost as though her muscles had taken a beating. In fact, her illusions had suffered the most — and her very good opinion of herself. She had been wrong about everything, from the time she had driven into the driveway and seen the purple thing with the green turban.

"I'll think about your advice, Mrs. Gibson," Dan said, and once again Alison could feel silent amusement shaking him. His right hand left the wheel and dropped to cover hers briefly.

She glanced sharply at him. The mirth had left his face, leaving only a shining gentleness.

Innocently, Mrs. Gibson prattled, "You always get what you want, Dan, even though sometimes it takes longer than I think it ought to."

Mrs. Gibson might well be right, Alison thought. Dan would always get what he wanted.

"We'll hurry back after the pageant is over," he said quietly to her. "We've got some research to do."

Blankly she looked at him. "Research?"

"The stable at midnight," he reminded her. "To see if the animals really talk."

She chuckled. "I really would like to hear what that black and white animal had on her mind, chasing me over the fence," she said with a show of indignation.

"Remember what I said once before — a dark stable, a pretty girl, and who knows what can happen?"

She pulled up her coat collar and snuggled more deeply into the comfortable corner of the seat. She glanced sideways at him. Suddenly the stable at midnight on Christmas Eve seemed a fine and logical place to be. She found she was smiling.

Who knew what could happen, indeed?

We hope you have enjoyed this Large Print book. Other Thorndike, Wheeler, and Chivers Press Large Print books are available at your library or directly from the publishers.

For information about current and upcoming titles, please call or write, without obligation, to:

Publisher
Thorndike Press
295 Kennedy Memorial Drive
Waterville, ME 04901
Tel. (800) 223-1244

or visit our Web site at:

www.gale.com/thorndike
www.gale.com/wheeler

OR

Chivers Large Print
published by BBC Audiobooks Ltd
St James House, The Square
Lower Bristol Road
Bath BA2 3SB
England
Tel. +44(0) 800 136919
email: bbcaudiobooks@bbc.co.uk
www.bbcaudiobooks.co.uk

All our Large Print titles are designed for easy reading, and all our books are made to last.